W.A. Sliver

Clouds

An original American comedy, in four acts

W.A. Sliver

Clouds
An original American comedy, in four acts

ISBN/EAN: 9783744781503

Printed in Europe, USA, Canada, Australia, Japan

Cover: Foto ©Andreas Hilbeck / pixelio.de

More available books at **www.hansebooks.com**

DE WITT'S ACTING PLAYS.

(Number 149.)

CLOUDS.

AN ORIGINAL AMERICAN COMEDY, IN FOUR ACTS.

BY FRED MARSDEN.

(W. A. SLIVER.)

AUTHOR OF "ALMA; OR, HELD IN BONDAGE," "NEMESIS; OR, SUNSHINE AND
SHADOW," "IN THE TOILS," "TRUMPS," "SILVER STAR," ETC., ETC.

AUTHOR'S EDITION.

ALL RIGHTS RESERVED.

TO WHICH ARE ADDED

A description of the Costume—Cast of the Characters—Entrances and Exits
Relative Positions of the Performers on the Stage, and
the whole of the Stage Business.

New-York:

ROBERT M. DE WITT, PUBLISHER,

No. 33 Rose Street.

DE WITT'S ACTING PLAYS.

☞ *Please notice that nearly all the Comedies, Farces and Comediettas in the followi: list of* DE WITT'S ACTING PLAYS" *are very suitable for representation in small Amateur The tres and on Parlor Stages, as they need but little extrinsic aid from complicated scenery expensive costumes. They have attained their deserved popularity by their droll situation excellent plots, great humor and brilliant dialogues, no less than by the fact that they are t most perfect in every respect of any edition of plays ever published either in the United Stat or Europe, whether as regards purity of the text, accuracy and fulness of stage directions ar scenery, or elegance of typography and clearness of printing.*

** *In ordering please copy the figures at the commencement of each piece, which indica the number of the piece in "* DE WITT'S LIST OF ACTING PLAYS."

☞ *Any of the following Plays sent, postage free, on receipt of price—1 cents each.*

Address,

ROBERT M. DE WITT,
No. 33 Rose Street, New York.

☞ The figure following the name of the Play denotes the number (Acts. The figures in the columns indicate the number of characters—M. mak F. *female.*

CLOUDS.

An Original American Comedy,

IN FOUR ACTS.

BY FRED. MARSDEN,

(W. A. SILVER.)

Author of "Alma; or, Held in Bondage," "Nemesis; or, Sunshine and Shadow," "Zip," "In the Toils," "Trumps," "Silver Star," etc.

AS FIRST PERFORMED AT MR. A. R. SAMUELL'S NEW PARK THEATRE, BROOKLYN, UNDER THE MANAGEMENT OF MR. THOS. E. MORRIS, SEPT. 15, 1873.

AUTHOR'S EDITION.

TO WHICH ARE ADDED,

A DESCRIPTION OF THE COSTUMES—CAST OF THE CHARACTERS—ENTRANCES AND EXITS—RELATIVE POSITIONS OF THE PERFORMERS ON THE STAGE, AND THE WHOLE OF THE STAGE BUSINESS.

———◆———

NEW YORK:
ROBERT M. DE WITT, PUBLISHER,
No. 33 ROSE STREET.

ORIGINAL CAST.

A. R. Samuell's New Park Theatre,
Brooklyn, Sept. 15, 1873.
T. E. MORRIS, Manager.

Hon. Walter Randall (an Ex-member of Congress)......Mr. T. J. HIND.
Ralph Randall (a Young New Yorker who *has* been to
    Paris)..Mr. W. E. SHERIDAN.
William Wimberly (a Gentleman from Chicago).........Mr. M. LANAGAN.
Fred Town (a Gentleman of Family on the confines of
    Bohemia)..Mr. JOHN W. NORTON.
Dr. Edward Lane (an Æsculapian on the sands of Jer-
    sey)...Mr. J. C. DUNN.
Mr. Billy Buddles (an Honest Man)....................Mr. M. W. FISKE.
Mr. Albery Sedley (a Member of the Y. M. C. A.)......Mr. OWEN MARLOWE.
Robert (a Servant)..................................Mr. JOHN P. COOK, Jr.
Stella Gordon (under a cloud)........................Miss ISABEL FREEMAN.
Cora Adair (who despises the past but utilizes the
    present)..Miss HELEN TRACY.
Ella Randall (a New York Belle with a tendency to
    "gush")..Miss KATIE MAYHEW.
Eola Wimberly (a Prarie Flower, innocent and young)..Miss GERALDINE STUART.
Miss Matilda Prim (a Jersey Maiden with a veneration
    for "Dorcas")...Mrs. E. M. POST.
Mrs. Malvernon (who sympathizes with youthful loves).Mrs. C. M. WALCOT, Sen.
Martha (an American Help)................................

SCENERY.

ACT I.—Light landscape backing. Set handsome cottage, L. H. Porch to the

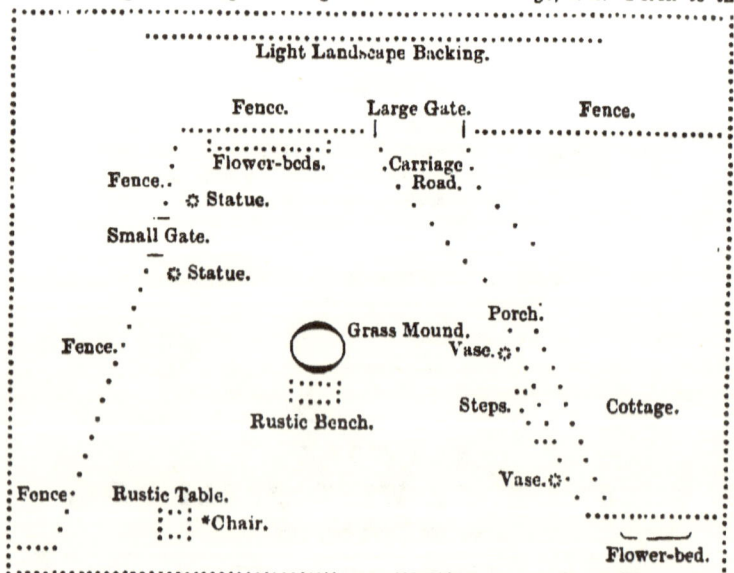

return covered with vines; vase of flowers R. and L. of porch steps. Run fence oblique from R. 1 G., up, and return off L. Small gate R.; carriage gate C. Round mound C., covered with grass, and on top a statue or fountain; rustic table and chair R. C.; rustic bench at mound, C. Flower-beds as in diagram. Canary bird in cage, hanging in porch. Garden cloth down, with carriage road leading off behind house. Set wings, oblique. Foliage borders. Statue or vase each side of gate, R.

ACT II.—Hudson river drop in 5. Set waters cross 4. Row boat, tied, C.; bank

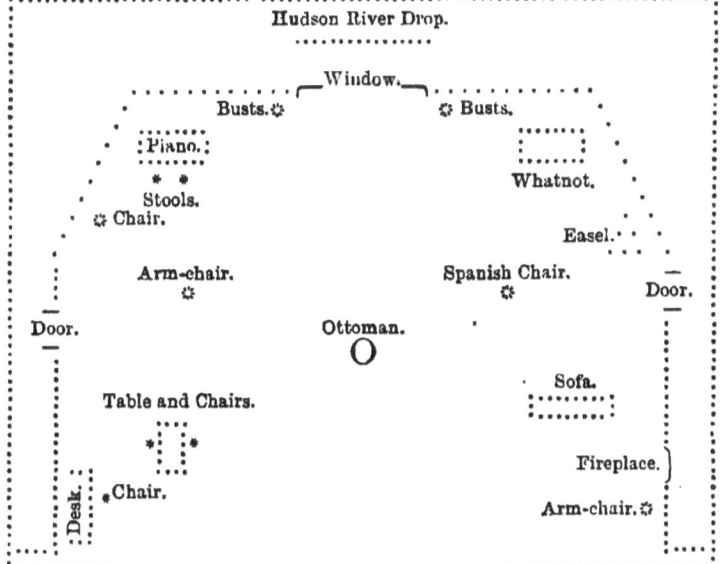

near boat; boat-house L. C.; tree R. H., with rustic table and chair: rustic seat below table, R. H.; two trees L. H., with a hammock swung between them; iron chair at head of the hammock; rustic bench at foot of hammock, L. H. Green baize down. Foliage borders; wood wings, oblique. Statues, bronze deer, etc.

ACT III.—Elegant drawing-room. Carpet down. Box set. Large window, opening on park, c., backed by Hudson river drop. Doors R. and L. Ceiling to room, with chandelier, not lighted. Handsome desk R. H.; table and chairs R. C.; large ottoman, ornamented with statue, in c.; piano and two stools, up U. H. corner; busts and pedestals R. and L. of window; handsome whatnot, up L. H. corner.; easel below it, with handsome painting or portfolio of engravings; rich sofa, L. H., near fire; arm-chair below fire; fireplace, down L. H., with grate fire burning; handsome mirror over mantel; Spanish chair up L. C.; arm-chair up N. C.; paintings on wall; large curtains to window; shovel and poker at fire; gong bell on table, R.

ACT IV.—Same as Act III.

SYNOPSIS.

ACT I.—Clouds on the Horizon. Scene.—Gordon Cottage, Eatentown, N. J. Tableau.—A Mother, but no Wife.

ACT II.—Watching in the Shadow. Scene.—Park of Mr. Randall's Villa on the Hudson. Tableau.—A Strange Proposal.

ACT III.—A Break in the Mists. Scene.—Drawing-room in Randall's House. Tableau.—The Betrayer and Betrayed.

ACT IV.—The Silver Lining. Scene.—Randall's Villa. Tableau.—Re-united Hearts.

PROPERTIES (See Scenery.)

Act I.—Garden cloth down. Written letter (No. 1) for FRED TOWN, and cigar and matches, in case; double-barrel shot gun, game-bag, shot-pouch and powder-flask, for RALPH; dog, for SERVANT; handsome work-basket, for MARTHA; glass of wine (blackberry) ready in house, for STELLA; written letter (No 2) for RALPH. Act II.—Baize down. Cigar-case, with cigar and matches, for WIMBERLY; book and blank letter with stamp on, for ELLA; boat oars in boat-house; handsome ladies' writing-desk and materials, for SERVANT to carry on. Act III.: Carpet down. See paper, pens, ink, envelopes, in desk, R., also account books, folded papers, and check-book (particular); music-book on piano; handsome books on table, R.; large pocket-book, for SEDLEY, containing a folded blank letter, in envelope; card photograph, for EOLA; rent receipt book, for BUDDLES; written letter (No. 3), for ELLA; blank letter, no stamp, for CORA. Act IV.: Carpet down. See gong bell on table, R.; Skein of Berlin wool, for EOLA; newspaper for WIMBERLY, with written paragraph; package of old letters, tied with white ribbon, neatly, for ELLA, also a package tied roughly with common string; written letter (No. 4), for ELLA; blank letter, no stamp, for WALTER RANDALL; small inlaid snuff-box, for FRED; old, faded marriage certificate, for STELLA.

STAGE DIRECTIONS.

R. means Right of Stage, facing the Audience; L. Left; C. Centre; R. C. Right of Centre; L. C. Left of Centre. D. F. Door in the Flat, or Scene running across the back of the Stage; C. D. F. Centre Door in the Flat; R. D. F. Right Door in the Flat; L. C. F. Left Door in the Flat; R. D. Right Door; L. D. Left Door; 1 E First Entrance; 2 E. Second Entrance; U. E. Upper Entrance; 1, 2 or 3 G. First Second or Third Groove.

R.   R. C.   C.   R. C.   L.

☞ The reader is supposed to be upon the stage facing the audience.

[For Synopsis of the Play, see pages 62, 63 and 64.]

CLOUDS.

ACT I.

SCENE.—*Cottage and grounds, Eatentown, N. J.* MARTHA *discovered on steps, fixing bouquet.*

MARTHA. There. now, I think that is just as sweet as can be—a rose, a lovely white bud, a dash of marguerite, a sprig of geranium, and some lake lilies. Oh, how I love flowers!

Enter MISS PRIM, *gate*, R.

How nice they look—just as pretty as a picture. I'm proud of this; what's the good of being a woman if you can't make a pretty bouquet?

PRIM (R. C., *sharply*). Martha!

MAR. (*starts violently*). Oh, my!

PRIM. What's the matter?

MAR. Good gracious, Miss Prim, you gave me such a shock.

PRIM (*sits* R). Did I? Pity you're so nervous. Where's your mistress?

MAR. Gone out. (*rises.*)

PRIM Where to?

MAR. Don't know, ma'am. (*pulls at flowers.*)

PRIM. When will she be back?

MAR. Don't know, ma'am.

PRIM. Where's your master?

MAR. Don't know, ma'am.

PRIM. Gone away again, I suppose?

MAR. Don't know, ma'am. (*fixes flowers in vase*, L.)

PRIM. Do you know anything, young woman?

MAR. Yes, ma'am.

PRIM. And what's that?

MAR. (*going up*). I know how to mind my own business, ma'am.

Enter DR. LANE, *gate*, R.

PRIM. And one thing more—you know how to be impertinent.

DR. LANE (*comes* C.). Well, Martha my girl, good day. Ah, Miss Prim, your most obedient. (*raises hat.*)

PRIM (*sharply*). Good day, doctor.

DR. L. You're looking quite yourself again. Rheumatism gone?

PRIM. Never had the rheumatism.

Dr. L. No? Bless me, I thought I heard so.

Prim. I was affected with a pain in my limb, and I consulted Dr. Pillby, a member of the church and a *reliable* physician.

Dr. L. Yes—and what did old Pill say?

Prim. *Dr. Pillby* said that the pain arose from a slight contraction of the ligaments of the limb, caused by a sympathetic affinity with the mental activity of my brain.

Dr. L. (*laughing*). Well, bless me, that's the most polite diagnosis I ever heard. Egad, I'll take lessons from my fashionable rival, and when I wish to speak of rheumatism again, I'll call it muscular contraction mentally accelerated. But come, this isn't business. Martha, how's my patient?

Mar. Nicely, doctor; he pulled my hair quite natural this morning.

Dr. L. That's a good sign. Where's your mistress?

Mar. Gone out, sir.

Dr. L. (*going* L.). That's a better sign; no doubt of his improvement now. Miss Prim, excuse me. (*aside*) Bless me, to think I came near marrying that woman once—ugh! [*Exit in house.*

Prim (*rises*). Martha, I can't wait here all day. Tell your mistress I called. I thought I'd be sure to find her home, as her child was sick.

Mar. (*up* c.). She is coming now, ma'am.

Music. Stella *runs on, gate,* R.

Stella. Well, Martha, here I am; did you think I'd run off for—— Oh, Miss Prim, is that you? I'm so glad to see you. How are you? (*kisses her*) I've just been having a good run; I've not been out before since baby was taken sick. But come in the house.

Prim (*stiffly*). No, thank you; Dr. Lane's there.

Stel. And you don't like him, do you? Well, sit down and we'll talk out here. I'm in such spirits this morning. Baby's so much better here, Martha, take in my things—he was very sick, you know. (Martha *takes things in.*)

Prim (*sits* R.). Yes; Mrs. Stubbs thought you'd lose him. He's not a healthy child.

Stel. He is rather delicate, but the doctor says he will be all right— the little darling. I'm so glad you came over. How's the rheumatism? (*sits on seat,* c.)

Prim. I wish you wouldn't talk like that. I'm not an old woman, to be down with rheumatism. Dr. Pillby assured me it was nothing of the kind.

Stel. I meant no offence; it's only my careless way of speaking. You know how giddy I am.

Prim. Yes, I do, more's the pity; you're too fond of the world.

Stel. We are all fond of it, Miss Prim, when we are happy. I'm just at the age, you know, when I can see beauty in everything. The chirping birds, the budding flowers, the rippling waters, all give me pleasure. I've nothing to be ashamed of in my past, and I'm contented in the present, and hopeful for the future. I like the world because I like to live. Ah, there's no sin in being happy!

Prim. That's what I call gush, and I've no sympathy with it. I've come to tell you I'm going away.

Stel. Going away!

Prim. Yes. My married sister has been worrying my life out to come and see her, and I'm going.

Stel. She lives in New York city, doesn't she?

Prim. If she did I'd never go near her while I had good sense.

Thank goodness, she lives up the Hudson, and not in such a sink of iniquity as New York.

STEL. But you will have to go through the city.

PRIM. Yes, but I'll ride through in a carriage, with the blinds down and a prayer-book in my hand. As I said to our minister last Sunday, don't talk to me about foreign missions ; send your missionaries to New York; it will be more beneficial and less expensive.

STEL. (*smiling*). Will you be gone long?

PRIM. I hope not; but while I am away I want you to take my place in the Dorcas Society.

STEL. I'm not a member.

PRIM. I know you're not; but you can join, I suppose.

STEL. Really, Miss Prim, you must excuse me.

PRIM. Excuse you ?

STEL. Yes ; I don't like Dorcas societies.

PRIM. Indeed. Why not ?

STEL. Because the members drink too much .ea and talk too much scandal.

PRIM. Thank you; I know where that comes from.

STEL. It comes from an earnest conviction, Miss Prim. I am willing to assist you in all your charities ; I will do any work you may assign me; but I simply request the privilege of doing it at home.

PRIM. Just what I expected. That husband of yours laughs at us, and is making you just as bad as he is. I'm sorry you let that worldly, careless man——

STEL. (*rises*). Your pardon, Miss Prim ; you are speaking of my husband.

PRIM. There, don't fly off; now that we're on the subject, I mean to do my duty and give you some advice.

STEL. (*pulls flowers in vase*, L.). If what you have to say concerns my husband, I would prefer not to hear it.

PRIM (*rises*). Well, it does concern him. Do you know people here are commencing to talk about Mr. Gordon?

STEL. Indeed ? Has Dorcas had him under consideration?

PRIM. Every one is wondering what sort of business he can have in New York, when he never goes there but he stays several weeks, and never comes back but he remains a month.

STEL. And the good people here are making his movements the subject of their earnest inquiries?

PRIM. Old Farmer Wells was in York some weeks ago, and he heard a man speak to your husband.

STEL. Indeed !

PRIM. And he called him by a different name than he is known by here.

STEL. (*slight start*). A different name? What was it.

PRIM. Old Wells don't remember; but he knows it wasn't Gordon. The farmer thinks, as he has another name in York, he may be one of them lottery chaps, or in——

STEL. (*turns*). That will do, Miss Prim. You are at liberty to speculate upon my husband's actions as much as you please, but I will feel obliged if you will not express your opinions to his wife. (*crosses*, R.)

PRIM (L. C.). Now don't be impulsive. A conscientious desire to do my duty——

STEL. (R.). There, Miss Prim, pray don't speak of duty. It is no one's duty to cast a shadow between a husband and his wife. It is this kind whispering of *friends* that often raises the first cloud between a happy couple, and has made of many lives a wreck that might have been a blessing.

PRIM. Gracious, my dear! I don't want to make any trouble. I wouldn't do that for the world. I only wish to warn——

STEL. Pray say no more. Let us drop the subject. It's not interesting, and might become unpleasant. (*sits*, R.)

FRED TOWN *sings outside.*

SONG.

In life I own it's very true
   Our joys are mixed with sorrow;
But keep a stout heart in your breast
   And never heed the morrow.
Your pockets may be empty, but
   A crust of bread's enough
To keep your legs in motion when
   They're made of the right stuff.

FRED (*appears* c.). I beg your pardon, but in the rural simplicity of this Arcadian retreat resides there a gentleman calling himself Gordon?

STEL. (*rises*). Yes, sir; this is his home.

FRED. Then I am right, and may venture to enter.

PRIM. A friend of your husband—I'll go. (*kisses* STELLA; *goes up, meeting* FRED, *who has entered a large gate*, L. C.)

FRED (*raises hat*). Have I the honor of addressing the sylvan goddess of this domestic Hesperides?

PRIM (*sharply*). Are you speaking to me?

FRED. I have that honor.

PRIM. Then speak English.

FRED. I will—is Mr. Gordon at home?

PRIM There's his wife—ask her. Good day.   [*Exit, gate*, R.

FRED (*raises hat*). Yours truly. (*aside*) If Xantippe was not dead, I'd think she'd left Greece and settled in New Jersey.

STEL. My husband went out this morning for some shooting. Have you any urgent business with him?

FRED (*down* L. C.). Oh, no, nothing particular. (*aside*) By Jove, I can't tell her! (*aloud*) The fact is, I was just passing, and dropped in, something on the Paul Pry order.

STEL. Who was he—a preacher?

FRED. Well, yes, in his way. He taught somewhat on the negative principle—illustrated the beauties of minding your own business by contrast.

STEL. Which implies——

FRED. That Paul Pry, by always interfering in other people's business, taught them the advantage of minding their own.

STEL Then, as you compare yourself to Paul Pry, you must be here on our business and not your own.

FRED. (*aside*). That's neat. (*aloud*) I came, my dear madam, to see Mr. Gordon, and have lingered too long. The charming beauty of this rural picture captivated me—a picture completed by the presence of a perfect object

STEL. And that is——

FRED (*raises hat*) Yourself!

STEL. Thank you; but the charming simplicity of the rural scene is, I think marred by one flaw.

FRED. And that is——

STEL. The presence of a flatterer.

FRED (*aside*). Egad! that's clever. (*aloud*) I cry you mercy, madam. I have a great admiration for your sex, but a wholesome dread of the one weapon nature has supplied them with—the tongue.

STEL (*crosses*, L.). Pardon me; we are wandering from the point. While waiting for Mr. Gordon, step in the house and let me offer you some refreshment.

FRED. No, thank you. (*aside*) I feel too much like a spy to eat at her table. (*aloud*) I'll just stroll around and smoke a cigar, and drop in again when Mr. Gordon returns.

STEL. May I know, then, who has honored us?

FRED. The honor is all on my side. I am simply a poor artist—a restless Bohemian. I see, admire, and reproduce. I know nothing of theory, ignore the romantic, live in an atmosphere of paints and brushes, and sacrifice high art to the vulgar accumulation of dollars and cents. The confession is sad but true, and so *au rivoir*. (*going*.)

STEL. Do you decline to leave your name?

FRED (*seriously*). Should fate ever throw us together when you may stand in need of the stout heart and strong arm of a friend, I will tell you all. Till then, adieu.   [*Bows and exits, gate,* R.

Enter DR. LANE, *from house.*

DR. LANE (*on steps*). Hoity toity! what's all this?

STEL. (*turns, sees him*). Why, my dear old friend, I forgot you were here. I've just had a visitor from the land of Bohemia, and he was quite interesting.

DR. L. (*coming down* L. C.). Humph! Bohemia is a subject to be let alone by the wife of a well-to-do young man. Who was that dandy?

STEL. He's an artist, and wanted me to sit for Venus. I refused, but offered to let him take a portrait of my bald-headed parrot. He got muffed, and departed with the prophetic warning, "We will meet again at Phillipi!"

DR. L. What are you going to Phillipi for?

STEL. My dear old Æsculapian, don't be stupid. I wished him to leave his name, but he refused and with the solemn accents of Hamlet's venerable papa, declared: "Should fate throw us together again I will tell you all; till then, adieu." So saying, he vanished.

DR. L. Let me feel your pulse.

STEL. (*laughing*). The impulse is upon me to repulse you; but I consider your age and so proceed

DR. L. (*takes her wrist*). Humph! slightly accelerated. You've got a little too much oxygen in the nervous system. A flow of spirits now—look out for the reaction.

STEL. Yes, that's the formula; I know it. Hold the wrist, count the pulse, roll up the eyes, look wise, say something no one can understand, pocket a fee, and leave Dame Nature to effect a cure.

DR. L. Bah! you trifle with serious things. What would people do if there were no doctors?

STEL. Adam and Eve got along well enough without one

DR. L. Nonsense! If Mother Eve had possessed a good family physician, it would have been much better for mankind.

STEL. How so?

DR. L. Why, the doctors would have told Eve that a green apple was indigestible, and she wouldn't have eat it.

STEL. The doctor would have done no such thing. He would have allowed Eve to eat the apple, so that if she got a colic he might get a fee.

Dr. L. Tut, tut! you jest on serious matters.

Stel. I was only carrying out your ideas. But there, I won't tease you, for you are a darling.

Dr. L. Ah, that's something like! When you state truisms, I'm silent.

Stel. I'll never forget you, my old friend, for to your care I owe my boy. His life was hanging by a thread; I knew it, and though I seemed calm, there was a seething volcano in my breast that nearly choked me. When I looked upon his sunken eye and hollow cheek, I could not weep—my grief could not find relief in tears; but when from the very brink of the grave you snatched him back to health and life, oh! it seemed as though the very excess of my joy caused pain. My soul was too full for thanks, but since that day, in my evening prayers for my boy, I have always breathed your name.

Dr. L. (*tries to hide emotion*). Hem! Let me feel your pulse. The reaction is about to set in; go in the house and be quiet.

Stel. I will; but don't go yet; I want you to have a nice glass of my home-made wine; I know you like that. (*crosses*, L) I won't be long. I'm going to get you some of the old blackberry, and that's an honor; I only give it to my very best friends.   [*Exit in house.*

Dr. L. (L. C.). That is a solid, substantial, good woman. A true wife and a loving mother deserves an honorable and upright man. I fear she has not got one. He is rich, without doubt; but no one can tell where his money comes from. Confound him, he's too secret to please me. I don't know why it is I dislike the fellow; his heart may be in the right place, but, damme, I'd like to feel his pulse.

Ralph Randall *enters gate*, R., *with gun, etc.; his servant passes behind fence, leading a dog, and entering at carriage gate*, L. C., *exits behind house.*

Ralph. Ah, doctor, you here? How are you—well?

Dr. L. Of course. Did you ever know me to be ill?

Ralph (*places gun on table*, R.). Never take any medicine, I suppose?

Dr. L. No, sir.

Ralph. That accounts for it. (*sits at table*, R.)

Dr. L. Did you have much luck?

Ralph (*in reverie*). Nothing to speak of. How's the boy?

Dr. L. On the sure road to recovery.

Ralph. No danger of a relapse?

Dr. L. Not the slightest.

Ralph. Thank Heaven for that; there's some comfort left me, anyhow.

Dr. L. You don't seem in good spirits.

Ralph. Think so?

Dr. L. Yes. Perhaps you're not feeling well?

Ralph. Perhaps not.

Dr. L. I may be able to help you; your nervous system appears shaken Hem! let me feel your pulse.

Ralph. Thank you, I'm not ill; when I am I'll let you know.

Dr. Lane *retreats*, L., Stella *re-enters, followed by* Martha *with handsome work-basket.*

Stella (*gives glass of wine*). There, doctor, drink that, and if you

don't say——(*sees* RALPH, *crosses*, R.) Why, Ralph, when did you come ?
I didn't look for you for hours yet. How good of you to come so soon.
There's nothing the matter, is there ?

RALPH. No—all the fault of the birds. They wouldn't come and be
shot, so I thought I might as well come home.

MARTHA (*on steps*). Do you want your basket now, ma'am.

STEL. Yes, put it on the table. How's the wine, doctor ? (MARTHA
places basket on table, timidly ; seems afraid of gun there.)

DR. L. (*starts from watching* RALPH). Splendid ! (*drinks hurriedly.*)

RALPH. If you'd take more time you'd find it more agreeable. (*rises,
saunters up* C.)

DR. L. That's true; there's a great many things done too hastily. But,
egad ! I must be off. (*crosses* R., *puts glass on table*) If all my visits were
this long my yearly income would not be encouraging. Good-bye, rose-
bud, take care of the nerves. (*aside, going*) If that man don't give her a
heartache yet, I'll never feel another pulse as long as I live!
[*Exit, gate,* R.

MAR. (*behind table*). Anything else, ma'am ?

STEL. No, thank you; you can go.

RALPH. (*comes* C.). Take my gun in.

MAR. (*nervously*). The—the gun, sir ?

RALPH. Yes, take it in the house. (*sits at mound,* C.)

MAR. I—I beg pardon, sir, but is—is it loaded ?

RALPH. Yes, but it can't hurt you; it has no cap on.

MAR. Yes, but sometimes they go off bareheaded.

RALPH. Oh, come, come, take it in and don't talk.

MAR. Yes, sir. [*Exit with it, very nervously, in house.*

STEL. (*comes to* RALPH). You tease, what did you make her do that
for ? you know how timid she is. But there, I won't scold you: you've
come home like a good boy, and you shall do just as you like. (*sits* L. *of
him.*)

RALPH (*yawns*). What have you been doing all day ?

STEL. I've been out—the first time since Willie was taken sick, you
know—and I've had such a run. I went to the store first, to see if I
could get some lace to match that you brought me ; you know how
afraid I was I couldn't get it ? Well. Mr. Mortimer had just the thing.
I saw old Lawyer Bradshaw there; he's coming over to-morrow evening
to play chess with you.

RALPH. Much obliged to him.

STEL. Then I went to Mother Gracie's—she was so glad to see me ;
and I left her some tea and some sugar, and a ham and potatoes, and—
don't laugh—some tobacco for her pipe.

RALPH. Wonderful.

STEL. Then I came home and found the doctor here, and Willie better, and I was in such spirits that the dear old man was frightened, and
said it was nervous force, and would be followed by depressed spirits.
You know he always thinks joy is followed by sadness.

RALPH. I suppose he frightened you ?

STEL. No, he didn't. I can never be sad while I have you and my
boy.

RALPH. Then I have made you happy ?

STEL. Happy? Why, Ralph, you have made my life so complete that
I almost forget I was once a poor girl. I'm woman enough to like good
clothes, and the people here are quite horrified at the way I dress ; they
say they never saw such goings on until we came. But I don't care
what they think or say. I dress to please you ; I want to keep on pleas-

ing you, Ralph—to make you love me more and more; for your love is my happiness.

RALPH. This happiness is so complete, then, I suppose a sudden grief would kill you?

STEL. I don't know—I don't like to think of that. If it concerned only me I might sink under it; but if it concerned those very dear to me I think I could meet the worst trouble face to face. But why do you ask?

RALPH. No reason—only a passing thought.

STEL. (*looks at him intently*). Ralph!

RALPH. Yes.

STEL. What's the matter?

RALPH. Nothing.

STEL. Then why don't you sit natural?

RALPH. I was thinking. There! (*puts arm around her.*)

STEL. I know a time when you didn't have to be told to do that.

RALPH. Oh, well, a fellow don't feel like courting after he's once married—a woman oughtn't to expect it.

STEL. Why not? Is the wife less worthy of attention than the maiden? A husband who really values his happiness should never let the fact of possession weaken his sense of what is due to the woman he has won. A man's conduct after marriage should at least be commensurate with his fervor before.

RALPH. That's nonsense! A fellow has to make so many vows to get a girl, that he deserves a little rest when she is won.

STEL. Yes, but they don't rest in the right way. They reserve their excessive courtesy for the ladies of society, and their wives have to receive the benefit of their *resting* at home.

RALPH. Have I ever troubled you by attentions to other women?

STEL. Well, you're away so much. You go to New York for weeks at a time, and I don't know what you do then.

RALPH. This is a new phase in your character, Stella; I thought you above jealousy. (*removes arm.*)

STEL. There, sit still. I was only teasing you, Ralph. I love you, and I could not love if I could not trust. I believe in you so fully that I will not believe a word against you.

RALPH. Some one *has* been talking, then?

STEL. Miss Prim was here.

RALPH. With her usual budget of news?

STEL. She is going away.

RALPH. Thank Heaven! If she leaves the state there may be some hope for New Jersey, after all?

STEL. She had news about you this time.

RALPH. Indeed! What was it—that I am a spendthrift, or that I don't go to church twice on Sundays?

STEL. (*laughing*). Oh, no, it wasn't that. I really don't know what it was—I refused to listen to her. It was something about your business in New York. She said you have a different name there from what you have here.

RALPH (*aside*). The inquisitive old hag! (*rises, crosses, L.*)

STEL. (*rises*). It's not true, Ralph, is it?

RALPH. True? What name did she mention?

STEL. None; the farmer who told her couldn't remember. She said you must be in a secret business. I would not listen to her, but I did not know how to defend you. I don't know what your business is myself. You stay here for weeks, then go away for a long time, and return with plenty of money. I don't want you to be angry, Ralph, but I've often wished you'd take me a little more into your confidence.

RALPH (*takes her hand*). Don't let us renew old subjects, Stella. I have told you there were some things in my life must remain secret.

STEL. (*sadly*). Yes.

RALPH. The business that takes me to New York is part of that secret, and I must request that you will not seek to penetrate it. When the time comes——Hush! there's some one coming up the walk. (*crosses c., looks R.*)

STEL. Who is it?

RALPH (*starts*). Great heavens!

STEL. What's the matter?

FRED TOWN *appears at gate, R.*

RALPH. Nothing; go in—I'll tell you when he's gone.

FRED. Mr. *Gordon*, I believe?

RALPH (*coldly*). Excuse me a moment, sir. Come, Stella, this gentleman and I have business. I must ask you to go in the house. (*leads her to steps.*)

STEL. It's no trouble, Ralph?

RALPH. No, no—don't fret.

STEL. (*aside, on steps*). There's something wrong—I'm *sure* of it. [*Exit in house.* RALPH *watches her off, then turns to* FRED, *who toys with work-basket on table.*]

RALPH (C.). Well, sir, how am I to regard you—as a spy or as a friend?

FRED (*at table, R.*). As neither. I could not descend to the *role* of a spy, and will no longer pretend to be your friend.

RALPH. In what character, then, do you pay this visit?

FRED. Simply that of ambassador.

RALPH. And what power sends so dignified a messenger?

FRED. Your father!

RALPH (*starts*). My father! then he knows——

FRED. *All!* (RALPH *sinks in seat, C*) I didn't want to do this thing; it looks like meddling; but——

RALPH. There, don't trouble yourself to apologize. You have been sent here by my father. Now, how did he know I had a place here?

FRED. I didn't know; I had not the slightest suspicion of it until he told me.

RALPH. Is it a part of your mission to conceal what you do know?

FRED. No. You have a right to all the explanation in my power. Your father sent for me a few days since, and I found him greatly agitated. He said he had just received a great shock, that he had been deceived in you, that you were not, as he thought, simply idling your time in New York, but supporting a country place upon his money, and acting the part of a vile, mean and base——

RALPH (*rises*). There, sir; spare your adjectives. (*crosses, R.*)

FRED. They are your father's—not mine.

RALPH (*sits R.*). As his agent I presume you endorse them?

FRED. I am his agent, as you are pleased to term it, because your father is too dear to me for me to refuse him a favor. I came here cheerfully, feeling there must be a mistake. I confess there is a mistake, but I regret to find I have made it. You are either to be very much pitied or very much condemned; in either case you have fallen from the high position in which my imagination placed you.

RALPH. I believe I am not accountable to you for my actions.

FRED. Every gentleman is accountable to his associates for an act inconsistent with honor.

RALPH (*rises*). Confound you, sir! what have you to do with my honor? How do you know what I have done, or intend to do? Has my father commissioned you to insult me, or is this gratuitous?

FRED. I have no intention of insulting you. Don't let us quarrel, Ralph. As men, don't let us forget we have been playmates. In that house there is a woman whom I believe to be too good and pure to suffer what I fear is in store for her; I want you to think of her *at any cost*, and be true to yourself

RALPH. Spare your comments, please, and confine yourself to business. You are here as agent, I believe, not as tutor. (*crosses*, L.)

FRED. Then, sir, as agent, permit me to place in your hands this letter. (*gives it*) In giving you this I execute, to the full extent, your father's instructions. In terminating my agency, permit me, sir, to add, that I trust this evening may also terminate our acquaintance.

[*Bows coldly, exits, gate*, R.

RALPH. That man despises me. I wouldn't let him see how his words affected me, but they went to my heart like a knife. Well, I suppose I have no right to complain. The world judges of a man by his actions, and never troubles itself about his motives. (*turning letter*) I wonder what the governor has to say? He's too fond of playing *le grande seigneur* not to take advantage, of this opportunity of reading me a lecture. I suppose it's a long-drawn homily upon morals. I wish I could afford to send it back unopened. (*suddenly opens letter*) Confound it! what's the use of speculating—let's know the worst. (*reads*) "To Ralph Randall, calling himself Ralph Gordon. Sir:—The honor of our family, which has in you received its first blemish, demands that we should have an explanation. When I inform you that I know all, you will have sufficient appreciation of my character to understand the consequences to yourself if you do not instantly follow the bearer of this missive. As your future very materially depends upon your present actions, I trust that personal considerations will so far influence your conduct as to mitigate in some degree, the contempt I experience upon being compelled to subscribe myself—your father." (*crushes letter*) Just what I expected. A cold, stilted, insulting letter; without one sign of heart in all its chilling diction. And yet this man wonders that I don't love him. Well, I'm not such a fool as Pygmalion to fall in love with marble.

MARTHA *enters from house*.

MARTHA. Mrs. Gordon is asking for you, sir.

RALPH (*starts*). All right; I'm coming—yet stay, Martha.

MAR. Yes, sir.

RALPH. Say I'm going into the library a few minutes to write a letter —then I'll come to her.

MAR. Yes, sir. [*Exit in house.*

RALPH. I've got to do it—the sooner the better. It's but one more infamy—I wonder if it will be the last?

Exit in house. It has been slowly coming on night, stage one-third dark.
BUDDLES *enters gate*, R., *comes down very cautiously.*

BUDDLES. That's the house; nice and comfortable—least it looks comfortable from the outside A pretty cage for a pretty bird. Sensible girl—feathered her nest well. Hem, I wonder if the male bird's around? Shouldn't altogether like him to see me here—he's got such an uncomforatble temper, and that's unpleasant. If he saw me I could he out of it—I've got so used to that now, it's almost a trouble to tell the truth. What a nice accomplishment that is—to tell a good lie— none of your half and halfers—none of your little white fibs, but a good, solid, substantial, unvarnished, downright lie. It's the secret of business success. The man who can't tell a good lie is sure to—(*starts, takes off hat*) I beg pardon; I just called—(*seeing no one*) As I'm an honest man, I thought some one pinched me. It's strange how uncomfortable I feel when I'm on strange ground. If anyone was to see me they might think I was prying—that would be a slur on my character. I hate prying—it's a mean, low, sneaky—(*starts*) Oh, lor'! the male bird *is* home.

Conceals himself behind vase, L., *as* RALPH *re-enters from house, with letter. Music, tremulo, pp.*

RALPH. I am trembling, like the coward I am. I never, until this moment, felt how utterly low and mean a man may become. Well, I have taught myself to expect this; now I must face it as best I can. What will she think of me when she reads this? Well, I won't think of that. There, she'll find you there quick enough (*places letter in work-basket on table,* R.) What a contrast! The pretty amusement of her idle hours covering the confession of my ignoble life! Well, so be it. The sting of the reptile is often covered by the fairest flowers. It is done, and I have no longer a place here. I have put the finishing touches to the greatest villainy of my life, and now—now I'll go to my father.

[*Exit, gate,* R.

BUD. (*comes out cautiously*). As I'm an honest man, he's a rascal. Good—ha! ha!—good! Suppose he'd caught me listening—damme, that would have been bad. He's left a letter for her; he's going away —going back to the old man. He must know we're on his track. I wonder if he's told all in that letter? That won't do—I came here to tell that myself. I'll just take charge of that letter—I will, as I'm an honest man. (*goes to table, takes letter.*)

STELLA *appears on steps.*

STELLA. What are you doing? (BUDDLES *turns, startled, concealing letter.*)

BUD. I beg pardon; I just dropped in.

STEL. (*comes down,* L. C.). Another Paul Pry. Well, sir, as it is somewhat late, and you are a stranger, will you kindly explain your business?

BUD. I will, ma'am, as I'm an honest man.

STELLA. What were you doing when I entered—my presence seemed to frighten you?

BUD. Frighten! Oh, no, madam, not frighten. I'm a man. But I had a misfortune, madam, in my youth. When I was a baby the nurse dropped me in a bucket of cold water, and I've never got over the shock to my nerves. (*aside*) That lie's weak, but it's too late to alter.

STEL. What made you start so when I spoke to you?

BUD. My nerves, madam. A voice suddenly striking upon my ear acts like a galvanic battery upon my muscles. It's a disease with me, ma'am. It's what I call an unnatural activity of the nervous system.

STEL. Well, sir, is this unnatural activity the cause of your being here?

BUD. No, ma'am, I came here to see you.

STEL. To see me! What for?

BUD. (*mysteriously*). To tell you something you should know.

STEL. Don't be so mysterious, please. If you have anything to say, speak out. You can say nothing that I am either ashamed or afraid to hear.

BUD. (*in low voice*). Are you sure?

STEL. So sure that I will instantly give you proof. (*turns L.*)

BUD. What are you going to do?

STEL. Call my husband that we may together listen to your communication.

BUD. Stop. It's about him I want to speak.

STEL. Then is there the greater need of his presence; to thank you if you speak well, to chastise you, if you speak false.

BUD. He won't thank me, as I'm an honest man; and he can't chastise me—for he's gone.

STEL. Gone!

BUD. Gone, as I'm an honest man. He knows the storm is coming, and he's trying to find shelter.

STEL. Gone—my husband gone!

BUD. The man who has——

STEL. Silence!

BUD. Yes, but I can prove——

STEL. Silence! A being like you shall not insult the man I love.

BUD. Yes, but he is——

STEL. No matter what he is or was. If my husband has been guilty of any wrong the knowledge of it shall not come to me first from the lips of a spy.

BUD. Won't you let me speak?

STEL. I have but one answer. Go! (BUDDLES *retreats behind table.*)

BUD. Well, then, if you won't hear me, listen to him. (*places letter on table. She takes it.*)

STEL. A letter! Why, it's Ralph's writing!

BUD. He told me to give it to you, but I hated to do it, as I'm an honest man. (FRED TOWN *appear at gate,* R. *Music, pp.*)

STEL. A letter; and Ralph gone! It must be that man. Oh, I knew he brought bad news. (*reads*) "My darling:—The spring is past, and the dreary waste of winter has come. No frost can ever chill my love, but the horizon of which you were the sun is now clouded forever. As low as a man can fall I have fallen. My life to you has been a deception, and I am now forced to fly. It will be useless to seek me, but, though away from you, I will amply provide for your future. How vile I have been these words will prove: Our marriage was not legal—you are not my wife." (*gasps*) "After so much deception, to speak the truth seems mockery, and yet my only truth has been, and is—my love. Ralph." (*after struggle turns calmly to* BUDDLES) I have had the courage, you see, to read this letter to the end.

BUD. You believe me now? (*comes down,* R.)

STEL. I *believe* this letter. You appear to know this man; who is he?

BUD. What do you mean?

STEL. I mean the man who called himself Ralph Gordon—what is his real name?

FRED (*comes down* C.). Perhaps I can best answer that question.

BUD. (*starts*). What! Fred Town!

FRED. I told you, madam, should fate throw us together again, that I would tell you my name. Fate has now answered your question. (*points to* BUDDLES.)

STEL. Fred Town?

FRED. Yes, madam, Fred Town, who has never yet had cause to blush for his bame, and who now, as a gentleman, appreciating your distress, begs you to accept his friendship.

STEL. Answer me one question—you must know all—who is Ralph Gordon?

FRED. The man who called himself Ralph Gordon is Ralph Randall, son of Walter Randall, of New York.

STEL. (*unnaturally calm*). Thank you—good night! (*going L., staggers.*)

FRED. You are ill! (*starts towards her.*)

STEL. (*motions him away*). Do not be alarmed—I am strong! I am a mother, and my child has only me now to protect his future. I will not faint—I will act.

FRED. What do you mean?

STEL. (*on steps*). I mean that I *am* this man's wife in the sight of heaven; I intend to make myself his wife in the sight of men. (*Calcium on her. Picture.*)

MEDIUM CURTAIN.

ACT II.

SCENE.—*Park of* MR. RANDALL'S *villa on the Hudson.*

Enter WALTER RANDALL *and* WILLIAM WIMBERLY, L. U. E.

WIMBERLY (L. C.). Delightful place, Walter, delightful; no disguising that fact. I don't blame you for being proud of your property.

RANDALL (R. C.). I believe I have every reason to be pleased. You have no scenery equal to this in Chicago.

WIM. Well—hem! no; that is, we have nothing so romantic; but then we have a sweep of prairie that is magnificent, if you could only get high enough to get a good look at it.

RAN. The best point of observation there would no doubt be a balloon.

WIM. (*takes out cigar case*). Look here, Walter, don't try to make fun of Chicago. Have a cigar?

RAN. Thank you, I never smoke. (*sits at table, R.*)

WIM. Chicago is the city of the future, sir—the city of push and go. Rapid thought there is followed by rapid action. We don't take fifty years to build a court-house, nor do we call every new party Reform, and oblige them to raise the taxes to pay off the extravagances of a defunct ring. (*lights cigar.*)

RAN. Why, you don't mean to say we have no push here?

WIM. Bless you, no. You've got push enough, but it's not of the right sort; your push is directed against one another, and the weaker party goes to the wall.

RAN. Why, I thought you were partial to our city.

WIM. Nonsense! that's my brother, Ben; you're thinking of him. He wasn't satisfied till he got to New York; bought that property out at Manhattanville, you know. He thought he had a fine thing, wrote me it was a big speculation, that rapid transit would soon be a practical fact, and his home be worth double what he gave for it. This was years ago. Now look at him: he hasn't got rapid transit, and he has got chills and fever.

RAN. I'm sorry to hear that.

WIM. I'm not, sir! serves him right—teach him a lesson. When a man has his foot upon solid ground he ought to feel——(*stamps foot, draws it up quickly*) The devil! (*staggers to seat down* L.)

RAN. (*rises, crosses to him*). What's the matter?

WIM. (*sits* L., *caresses leg*). Gout, sir, gout! Yankee's showing fight.

RAN. Yankee?

WIM. Yes. Ever since the war I've called one foot rebel and the other Yankee, and when the gout comes, damme, how they do fight! (*holding foot*) Yankee's got the best of it just now.

RAN. You should put the Palmetto on one boot and the Union Jack on the other.

WIM. What for?

RAN. To keep you from forgetting. (*sits in chair,* L)

WIM. Forgetting! Well, if ever you get the gout I'll go bail you won't forget it. It telegraphs its presence as soon as it arrives, and keeps the brain posted as to what's going on in the foot.

RAN. I have fortunately been spared the affliction, but I can form some idea of its severity from the description of others. It serves a purpose, though—warns men against an epicurean career.

WIM. Damn it, Walter, don't preach! Gout's bad enough without a sermon. This is only a twinge now, but if Yankee really means fight, I'll be forced to pay you a longer visit than I intended.

RAN. Don't speak of that. I will regret your suffering, but be happy to prolong your stay with us.

WIM. Thank you.

ELLA RANDALL *and* EOLA WIMBERLY *enter,* L. U. E , *arm in arm.* ELLA *has a book and blank letter ;* EOLA *goes down to her father.*

ELLA. I have been looking for you, papa; here's a letter.

RAN. Thank you. With your permission, William. (*rises, crosses* R., *sits at table, reads letter ;* ELLA *goes up.*)

WIM. Well, miss, what have you been doing?

EOLA (*at his knee*). Throwing pebbles in the water.

WIM. Bless me! that's nice amusement—what for?

EOLA. To make rings.

WIM. Oh, I see! You've caught the New York fever already.

EOLA. What's that, papa?

WIM. Making rings. You can't help it, my child; it's in the atmosphere here, and——ah, look out! don't touch my foot.

EOLA. A battle?

WIM. No; only a skirmishing party.

EOLA. Which is it, papa—rebel?

WIM. No, Yankee; and he's in a precious bad humor. But, I say, Walter, any bad news?

RAN. (*starts from reverie*). On the contrary, my son returns to-day. (*rises.*)

WIM. Glad to hear it.

ELLA (*runs down* R. C.). What's that, papa—Ralph coming?

RAN. This letter announces that fact.

ELLA. Oh, that's jolly! (*looks at* RANDALL, *startled*) I mean delightful.

WIM. You don't see much of your brother, eh?

ELLA. Hardly see him at all, and when he does come he's not like himself. He used to be the life of the place, and when he went away it was awful.

RAN. (*sternly*). If young ladies would take the trouble to understand the *meaning* of the words they use, they would give the word *awful* a rest.

WIM. Why, bless me, Randall, you're using slang.

RAN. I had no intention of doing so. But come, if Yankee will permit you; I've not shown you all the beauties of my place yet.

WIM. Wait till I see. (*rises, places foot down carefully*) Ah! All quiet upon the Potomac. I guess I'll venture. But don't go far; it won't become your dignity to bring me back on your shoulders.

RAN. (*gives his arm*). I'll risk that.

WIM. Now then, you girls, look out; we're going to leave you alone; don't get in any mischief. [WIMBERLY and RANDALL *exeunt*, R. 3 E.

ELLA. We won't. Ah! they're gone at last; what a relief. These fathers are awful bores, ain't they? (*crosses, sits L.*)

EOLA. My papa's not a bore.

ELLA. That's so—he's jolly; but my governor's slow—one of the awful solemn kind. Why, if he was riding behind one of Bonner's best, the only sensation he'd have would be the fear of falling out. But come, sit down and let's have a nice talk.

EOLA (*sits beside her on seat*, L.). Why, don't you love your father?

ELLA. Love him? Of course; but I don't gush about it. Papa's stern and dignified, and that's why he and Ralph can't get along together. Ralph used to be so jolly.

EOLA. Your brother does business in New York, doesn't he?

ELLA. What! Ralph do business? Why, bless your little innocent soul, Ralph has no more idea of business than my canary has of making love.

EOLA. Then, why does he live in New York?

ELLA. Because he can spend money there faster than he can here. He does as he pleases there—we don't even know where he lives; we send our letters to his club. Papa's been very angry with him lately, though. These fathers are awful disagreeable sometimes, but one can't well do without them—at least, until we're married.

EOLA. Oh, dear! how you talk.

ELLA What's the matter?

EOLA. My papa don't like me to talk about marriage; he says young girls shouldn't think of such things.

ELLA (*in great surprise*). Why, bless me! what else has a young girl got to think about?

EOLA. Papa says it's time enough for me to think about it when I'm a grown-up woman.

ELLA. Pshaw! Why, your father's worse than mine. Now, you look out; if you wait until you're a grown-up woman, you'll end by becoming a ringleted old maid, and die in solitude, lamented only by the cats.

EOLA. I wouldn't like to be an old maid.

ELLA Then make hay while the sun shines. Matrimony's the hay, and youth's the sunshine. Study the men—they need it. They're precious artful, and the more you study them the more you'll be puzzled. But you're a woman, and if you only keep your wits clear and your heart firm, you can rule the best man that ever breathed.

ELLA. Papa don't like me to talk much to young men.

ELLA. Oh, bother! your father don't understand these things—fathers never do. It's natural; they've out-grown it. Now, just thing of it. When they're in petticoats they play with dolls; when they sport their first boots, they kick football and gamble in marbles; when they go to school they fall in love, and when they get an income they marry. The first child they spoil, the second they scold, and the third they grumble at; and by the time they have worried all the hair off their heads and wear a wig, they talk politics and philosophy, and forget they were ever young.

EOLA. My papa's not like that.

ELLA. Well, come ; when did your father marry ?

EOLA. He was married twice.

ELLA. And now he don't want you to marry once.

EOLA. Oh, no ! he don't mean that; he only want's me to know a man's character well first.

ELLA. Well, how are you going to know anything about if you don't talk to him ? You can't study a man's character by looking at his photograph.

EOLA. No, I don't think you can.

ELLA (*both rise*) Well, now, you take my advice, and I'll make you profit by this visit ; and when you return to Chicago you'll be fully accomplished. I'll teach you—(*looks* R.) Oh, dear !

EOLA. What's the matter ?

ELLA. Here comes my shadow—young Modest.

Enter ALBERY SEDLEY, R. 1 E.

Good-day, Mr. Sedley ; you're just in time—we were talking of you.

SEDLEY (R. C., *raises hat*). Anything bad ?

ELLA (C.). No, indeed ; we were saying lots of nice things. Let me present you to my friend, Miss Wimberly, Mr. Albery Sedley.

SED. Delighted, I'm sure.

ELLA. Now mind, I won't have you tease her, if she is from the country.

SED. The country ? Why I thought Miss Wimberly was from Chi- , cago ?

ELLA. Well, so she is ; but you don't call that little western town, with its plank sidewalks, a city, do you?

SED. I'll call it a wilderness, if you wish it.

ELLA. Did you come to take me out boating ?

SED. I expected that pleasure.

ELLA. Well, I can't go ; I'm busy.

SED. Indeed ?

ELLA. Yes, sir; indeed. But I'll take pity on you, and send a substitute.

SED. Miss Wimberly ?

EOLA (L. C., *aside to* ELLA, *pulls her dress*). Oh, no, no !

ELLA. Yes. Miss Wimberly is very fond of the water, and has been wishing all day for a sail.

EOLA (*aside to her*). Why, Ella !

SED. Be delighted, I'm sure.

CORA ADAIR *enters* L. U. E., *followed by* SERVANT, *with writing-desk.*

CORA (*crosses* R.). Good-day, Mr. Sedley. Put the desk, on the table, Robert. Have you been rowing ? (*sits at table,* R.)

[SERVANT *places desk on table. Exits,* L. U. E.

SED. Just about to start. (*to* ELLA) I'll get the oars. (*goes up, enters boat house.*)

EOLA. Oh, Ella, what have you done ? I can't go without you.

ELLA. Nonsense, don't be silly.

EOLA. I know papa will not like it.

ELLA. You follow your father's advice and you'll die an old maid ; follow mine, and you'll die a rich widow.

EOLA. But I don't want to marry this man.

ELLA. Well, Miss Innocent, you don't have to marry a man because you go boating with him.

SED. (*comes out with oars*). Quite ready, Miss Wimberly. Will you join us, Miss Adair ? (ELLA *leads* EOLA *up.*)

CORA (*writing at desk*). No, thank you. I'm too deep in correspondence to think of pleasure.

SED. Permit me. (*helps* EOLA *in boat.*)

EOLA (*totters*). Oh ! look out.

SED. All right, not the slightest danger. (*to* ELLA) I do wish you had gone.

ELLA. Oh, pshaw, get in and row the boat. (*they row off* R.) Good bye, Eola, take care your dress don't get wet. (*comes down laughing*) Poor child, she looks as frightened as if she were going to prison.

CORA (*writing*). Why did you not join them ?

ELLA (*sits on seat*, L., *reads*). Because I wanted to read Middlemarch ; I'm just getting interested.

CORA. In what character, Casaubon ?

ELLA. I should think not ; there's too much parchment about him for me ; I like poor Dorothy, but I skip her husband. I suppose he's your favorite.

CORA. By no means. He was a failure, and I despise a failure.

ELLA. I'm just reading where Fred Vincy made that mistake in his horse trade. Poor Fred, he's jolly—I love him.

CORA. Speaking of Freds—that reminds me, I received a letter from Mr. Town this morning.

ELLA (*starts*). Indeed !

CORA. Here it is—you can read it.

ELLA (*throws book on seat, rises*). Read his letters to another woman ? Oh no, thank you.

CORA. It is simply upon business.

ELLA (*quickly*). And what business has he to write--(*stops, turns away confused*) Oh, pshaw !

CORA. I will tell you its contents.

ELLA. Don't trouble yourself. (*sits on hammock, swings.*)

CORA. Mr. Town simply informs me, that he will return to-day, and present the new housekeeper.

ELLA. The new housekeeper ?

CORA. Your father desired him to bring one up from the city, if he could find a suitable person.

ELLA (*rises*). And why didn't my father tell me of this ?

COBA. Excuse me, dear, but your father is the proper one to answer that question.

ELLA. And he shall answer it ; I'm not going to be made a nonentity here, if I'm not as old and wise as *some people*.

CORA. Do you refer to me ?

ELLA. N-o-o.

CORA. Your father loves you too well to refuse you an explanation.

ELLA. You seem to understand my father better than I do.

CORA. I understand that you are provoked because Mr. Town has written me a letter, and permit yourself to speak without reflection.

ELLA. Provoked because Fred—I mean Mr. Town—wrote to you ? Well, that's nice. I suppose he can write to whom he pleases ; I'm not young enough to be surprised at anything a man does. (*sits* L., *reads.*)

CORA. I'm glad to hear it.

Enter FRED TOWN, R. U. E.

FRED. Ah! good day—ladies—I salute you. What a charming picture —living charms, rivalling the inaninate surroundings of nature.

CORA. You have returned ?

FRED. As you see ; the gods have been propitious, and I return in safety with my sketch book full and my pocket-book empty.

CORA (*seals a letter*). For all of which you are duly thankful.

FRED. Thankful *!* Why just think of it. I have been in New York and have neither been kidnapped, robbed nor murdered ; and returned on the Hudson River Railroad, and encountered no accident. Thankful ! I should say I was.

CORA. We are glad to see you.

FRED. Thanks—but apropos—I have a companion, the lady I informed you of, the custodian of your keys and manipulator of your servants, who is willing to guarantee you a *propre ménage* and waits without your gracious leave and pleasure.

CORA. Pray present her.

FRED. I will. By the way, where's Buddles ?

CORA. At the house, I suppose—why ?

FRED. Nothing. (*to* ELLA) Look here, you haven't said a word to me, Jap ; what's the matter ?

ELLA (*throws down book. rises*). My name's not Jap, sir. (*crosses* R.)

FRED (*aside, going up*). Humph ! something wrong. (*speaks off*, R. U. E.) Come this way, Mrs. Lee.

Music.— Enter STELLA, *slowly*, R. U. E.

Miss Adair, let me present to you Mrs. Lee. I am sure you will make her feel at home. (*aside to* STELLA) Keep up your courage, I'll go for Buddles. (*aloud*) Now, ladies, I must ask you to ecxuse me.

CORA. Are you going ?

FRED. I'm going to the house a moment, to see Buddles.

CORA (*looks closely*). You appear greatly interested in him ; have you any bad news ?

FRED. No—I have simply a drawing for him. (*aside*) That's true, I mean to draw his teeth. [*Exit*, L. 3 E.

CORA (*coldly to* STELLA). What is your name ?

STEL. Amy Lee.

ELLA (*sits* R. *of table* R.). What a pretty name.

CORA. You are married ?

STEL. I—I am—a widow.

ELLA. Poor dear, how romantic.

CORA. I presume you are accustomed to the duties of housekeeping ?

STEL. Yes—on a small scale.

CORA. Have you never had the care of a large household ?

STEL. No, madam.

CORA. In that case, how can you expect to give satisfaction.

STEL. I am very quick to learn, and although it may be a little strange at first, I will try so hard to please, that I am sure I will succeed.

CORA. From the tone of Mr. Town's letter, I scarcely expected he wished us to submit to an experiment.

STEL. I am not aware how far Mr. Town's desire to serve me may have carried him ; but I have told you simply the truth, I have not had large experience, but I will strive hard to give you satisfaction, if you will give me a trial.

ELLA. Why, of course we will.

CORA. Excuse me, Ella, I am acting in your father's interests. I have no desire to deal harshly with you, madam, but the position is a very responsible one, and—— ·

ELLA. Oh, pshaw ! Where's the responsibility ? keep the keys, give out the tea and sugar, regulate the butler, look after the silver and linen, and take a nap in the afternoon. There it is, in a nutshell. (*goes up.*)

CORA. I was about to observe that the responsibility of the position justified us in demanding unquestionable references.

STEL. Of course—I am quite prepared for that. (*aside*) Oh, this is torture.

CORA. The proper judge of this matter will, however, be Mr. Randall. (*looks* L.) I see Mr. Buddles coming, he can show you to the house for the present.

STEL. (*down,* C., *aside*). Buddles coming—now for the test. If he speaks, I am lost.

Enter BUDDLES, L. 3 E.

BUD. I saw Mr. Town—he sent me here—said you might want me.

CORA. I did not want you, but now that you are here, show Mrs. Lee there, to the house.

BUD. Very good. Hem. At your service, madam. (*stands* R. C.)

STEL. (*with back to him, aside*). Heaven, how I tremble !

BUD. When you're ready , ma'am.

STEL. I am quite ready. (*turns.*)

BUD. (*starts*). Bless me.

STEL. (*aside*). Lost.

CORA. What's the matter, Mr. Buddles ? do you know Mrs. Lee?

BUD. Know her ? Why bless me I never saw her before, as I'm an honest man.

CORA. Then, what surprised you ?

BUD. Her face—it's so calm—so sweet—so lovely.

CORA. There, that will do—show the woman to the house.

ELLA (*comes quickly down,* C.). This *lady*. Mr. Buddles, will remain here as housekeeper ; I will show her the house—you can go.

BUD. Very good. Don't mind me, Mrs. Lee, I'm only an humble man. (*aside, crosses,* L.) Ha ! ha—I frightened her, I kept my word with Mr. Town, but I frightened her. Never saw her before in all my life. Capital lie, as I'm an honest man.   [*Exit,* L. 1 E.

ELLA. You mustn't mind that old dunce, he's papa's man of business, and half crazy, I believe. Come, I'll show you your room.

STEL. Thank you. (*to* CORA) Shall I receive any orders ?

CORA. It is to save that trouble that you are here.

Enter MRS. MALVERNON *and* RANDALL, R. U. E.

MRS. MALVERNON (*as she enters*). No you won't, I'll not have it ; my favorite must be respected. How do you do, dear ? (*goes down* C., *kisses* ELLA) Your father wants to scold you, and I'm going to be the good fairy. (*bows to* CORA) Excuse me, Miss Adair, I was so anxious about Ella, it has made me impolite.

ELLA. What have I done now ?

RAN. (L. *of* CORA). Something that, notwithstanding my knowledge of your thoughtless nature, I confess, surprises me.

MRS. M. (C.). There, now, don't be severe. I'll tell you all about it, pet. You see, Mr. Wimberly saw his little Eola rowing on the river with a young man—he was horrified, and he waved his hat frantically until the young man rowed ashore and took him on board.

RAN. I, of course, knew it was your work, Ella, and, I assure you, it gave me no pleasure; I will speak to you, however, at a more fitting time. May I ask to be presented to your friend?

CORA. That is Mrs. Lee, who applies for the posi of housekeeper. She has been presented by Mr. Town.

MRS. M. My good-for-nothing nephew. So he has returned. Of course he came here first—eh, puss? (to ELLA.)

RAN. (raises hat). I am glad to see you, madam. (STELLA bows.)

CORA. I have not yet had an opportunity of seeing her references.

STEL. Mr. Town has them, sir; he wished to show them to you himself. I am sure you will find them satisfactory.

RAN. Your appearance, madam, is sufficient guarantee of your claim to our respect, and being presented by Mr. Town, ensures you a welcome. But we have detained you. Ella, Mrs. Lee may be fatigued. (goes up.)

ELLA. We're going.

MRS. M. One moment, dear, and I'll go with you. Miss Adair, I only ran over to let you know my visitor has arrived, and ask you to call.

CORA. I will take great pleasure in making the acquaintance of your friend. (goes up to RANDALL.)

ELLA. Is it your sister, Mrs. Malvernon?

MRS. M. Yes, puss, it's my sister—and be careful how you mention it; she's an old maid.

ELLA. Oh, dear! I won't like her!

MRS. M. And she comes from New Jersey. (STELLA starts.)

ELLA. Gracious! that's worse yet! She'll never be able to sleep here.

MRS. M. Why not?

ELLA. Jersey people never get any rest unless they're sung to sleep by mosquitoes.

MRS. M. Hush, you tease! Don't you let Miss Prim hear you speak against New Jersey.

STEL. (aside). Miss Prim!

ELLA. Gracious, what a name!

MRS M. Well, I've heard worse names than that.

ELLA. So have I. I heard of a man once who had such an ugly name the minister fainted trying to christen him.

MRS. M. Go along, you torment. I must really beg your pardon, Mrs. Lee, but when I get talking to my favorite here, I forget myself.

STEL. Pray don't mind me. (to ELLA) You go with your friend—I will follow you. (MRS. MALVERNON and ELLA exeunt, L. 1. E.) Miss Prim here! another obstacle. Heaven help me; it seems like fate.

[Exit, L. 1 E.

RAN. (comes down with CORA). I received this letter this morning. I am expecting him every minute

CORA (R. C.). I am very glad of it, for your sake; it gives you pleasure to have him here, and he comes so seldom.

RAN. (L. C.). It is all my fault, Cora—I have been, in a great measure, to blame for it. The truth is, Ralph has had too much his own way. I have occupied my mind with home matters, and the boy has run wild.

CORA (sits R.). Your son may be a little wild, but I wouldn't be too severe with him. It's somewhat difficult for a young man to resist the contagion of New York. He is fond of life, and—I suppose it's very improper to say—but I like him the better for it.

RAN. There is nothing puritanical in my nature, Cora, as you well know; but, while I believe in a young man seeing life, I do not believe in excess. Now Ralph, I am sorry to say——

CORA (rises quickly). Excuse me; don't betray his secrets

RAN. Yes, but Cora, this is something that you have a right to know.

CORA (*timidly*). Then let me hear it first from his lips. If your son ever speaks to me in the way you would have him speak, he will then, I am sure, tell me all that I ought to know.

RAN. (*takes her hand*). Bless you, my child; you seek to spare me even a blush My son will speak to you in the way I would have him speak, and he comes here to-day for that purpose.

CORA (*represses a start of joy*). There is only one thing that troubles me. I fear that—that your son feels rather forced into this.

RAN. Not at all; he don't know his own mind. But in any case, I do not intend to study his inclinations. It must suffice to him that it is my will.

CORA. Still, that is not very complimentary to me.

Enter BUDDLES, L. 1 E.

RAN. Well, what is it?

BUDDLES. Mr. Ralph, sir—just arrived—looks well and hearty—anxious to see you, as I'm an honest man. (*goes up.*)

RAN. I told you—he's prompt. Will you go with me?

CORA. No; you had better see him first.

RAN. Always considerate. Bless you, Cora; you are dear to me as my own child. I will see Ralph at once, and not neglect your happiness. (*aside*) Now to brace my nerves; there'll be a struggle, but I must win.

[*Exit*, L. 1 E. CORA *stands* R., BUDDLES *looks around, slowly comes down close to* CORA.

BUD. (*pointedly*). Well, he's come.

CORA (*with back to him*). So I perceive.

BUD. It's all right—he's up at the house—everything's going nice. You'll be Mrs. Randall after all.

CORA. Perhaps.

BUD. Perhaps? Well I wish I was as sure of being president. Why, the old man will——

CORA (*turns, crosses* L.). There; spare your comments; I'm not interested in your opinions.

BUD. Yes, but I'm interested in your acts, as I'm an honest man. I've found out all you wanted to know—I've put the old man on his son's track. Now keep your promise.

CORA. I will—in good time.

BUD. The best time is present time. You've got your foot on my neck; I want you to take it off. The sensation is not nice, as I'm an honest man.

CORA. I find nothing to complain of.

BUD. Of course not. A man's neck is softer than the ground.

CORA. Listen to me, please. I have known you too long not to understand you. Through me you obtained a position here that enabled you to worm yourself into your employer's confidence.

BUD. (*ironically*). How good of you—how charitable!

CORA. Don't interrupt me. I'll disguise nothing even from myself. I was *forced* to bring you here, I admit, but you were not forced to commit a crime.

BUD. It—it was a mistake.

CORA. But I hold a paper that would send you to answer that mistake in prison.

BUD. You wouldn't dare—*for I would speak.*

CORA. True—we are in each other's power—silence for silence. When I no longer dread you I will give you your release.

BUD. And that will be——

CORA. When what I came here for is accomplished—when I am Ralph Randall's wife.

Turns, sees ELLA, *who enters, sullenly,* L. 1 E.

Ah, Ella, has your brother come?

ELLA (*sharply*). Yes, he's come. (*crosses,* R.)

CORA. Mr. Buddles was just telling me that he had arrived, but I thought he must be mistaken   You must excuse me for doubting you, Mr. Buddles, and accept my thanks for your information.

[*Bows ; exit,* L. 1 E. *He looks after her.*

BUD. (*aside*). Well, if that woman had been in Eden the serpent wouldn't have had a show. (*to* ELLA) Miss Ella——

ELLA. Don't bother me.

BUD. Oh! I beg pardon—I thought——

FRED TOWN *enters, sullenly,* L. 1 E.

Ah, good evening, sir. I fixed that little——

FRED. Don't bother me. (*goes up.*)

BUD. Well, if I stay here much longer, I'll have my feelings hurt. There's something wrong ; I'd like to find it out ; but I wouldn't stoop to spy, as I'm an honest man.   [*Exit,* L. 1 E.

ELLA *crosses,* L., *sits on bench, takes up book ;* FRED *comes down slowly to her. Night comes on.*

FRED (*leans on back of seat*). Quite interesting, isn't it?

ELLA. Are you speaking to me?

FRED. Yes. I suppose your book's quite interesting.

ELLA (*reading*). If it were not why should I read?

FRED. Well, from the way you rushed at it, I thought you sought a refuge.

ELLA. From you?

FRED. Yes.

ELLA. Even a dull *book* is preferable to a dull companion.

FRED. Is it? (*yawns*) I wish I had a book.

ELLA (*rises, crosses* R.). If you find my society so dull I would advise you to leave.

FRED (*reclines in hammock*). Thank you ; I'm comfortable now. This is delightful.   This is a luxury Epicurus would have envied, and Anacreon immortalized.   In such a calm attitude of repose, Petrarch might have mused upon his Laura, or Alcibiades quaffed the juice of the grape, while the balmy zephers of the Ionan Isles chased each other through his curly locks.

ELLA (R.). Dear me, how poetical. Placing your body in repose appears to elevate your mind to the clouds.

FRED. There's everything in position. Your side to an opponent in a duel, your knee to a lady in a quarrel. Imagine the knee, please ; the soft air of the declining day has made me lazy.

ELLA. If I am any judge of character, that appears to be your normal condition.

FRED. All right—run through the list of my sins, and I'll reply with *mea culpa,* and end with Hamlet's plaintive cry, "Nymph, in thy orisons, be all my sins remembered?"

ELLA. Thank you; I've not the courage for such a task, and prefer leaving you to reflect on them. *(crosses, L.)*

FRED. Are you going?

ELLA. Yes. *(stands L. 1 E.)*

FRED. Well, if you meet Mrs. Lee, will you kindly tell her to make haste, or I'll fall asleep?

ELLA *(starts).* Mrs. Lee?

FRED. Yes—the housekeeper, you know—she wants to see me before I go. *(yawns)* I wish she'd hurry.

ELLA. You're greatly interested in your protege.

FRED. Yes—somewhat.

ELLA. Young widows are very romantic.

FRED. Yes, they are.

ELLA. Especially when they're handsome and poor.

FRED. Yes, that adds a charm. By the way, when you go——

ELLA. I'm not going. *(crosses, C)*

FRED. Ah, in that case never mind.

ELLA You're awful anxious to get rid of me.

FRED. Not at all; but you've been so angry with me I thought you wanted to get rid of me.

ELLA. I've not been angry. *(draws slightly near him.)*

FRED. Oh yes, you have.

..ELLA *(still nearer).* I—I wasn't angry—only annoyed.

·FRED. Why?

ELLA *(nearer).* Why—because—because——

FRED *(sits up).* Because what?

ELLA *(at head of hammock).* Well, because—because—Oh, you know very well.

FRED. Because you thought me a silly moth, singeing my wings in a new flame. *(puts arm around her.)*

FLLA *(draws away).* Well, when a girl is engaged to a man, she can't be expected to enjoy his flirtation with another woman.

FRED *(rises).* Wants all his attentions for herself, eh?

ELLA. Well, as she can't expect many from the husband, she ought to get all she can from the lover.

FRED *(sits down, L. H.).* Well, come here and be a good girl, and I'll tell you all about it.

ELLA. I don't want to. *(gets near him.)*

FRED. Oh, very well. *(about to recline on bench.)*

ELLA. There, don't be lounging about like that. *(sits.)*

FRED *(puts arm around her).* That's nice—now don't be cross any more.

ELLA. If Mrs. Lee comes——

FRED. Mrs. Lee is not coming.

ELLA. Why, you said so.

FRED. It was a fib. There's another sin to remember in your orisons.

ELLA. Well, what made you say so.

FRED. To teaze you for snubbing me so. Here I've just returned, and you've hardly noticed me, but raised your little eyebrows, and played offended Juno, with icicles hanging all around you.

ELLA. Well, you deserve it; away a whole two weeks, and only wrote me seven letters.

FRED. Well, that was bad, but I ran short of postage stamps.

ELLA. Then look at the way you came back, with a young woman.

FRED. There—don't fly off—she was in distress, and I helped her.

ELLA. You're *sure* you don't care anything for her ?

FRED. Perfectly.

ELLA. And you feel no interest in her ?

FRED. Well, only a certain sympathy.

ELLA. Never mind that—I'll sympathize with her.

FRED. Very well.

ELLA. And you were only joking when you said she was coming out here.

FRED. Positively !

ELLA. On you honor, sir ?

FRED. On my honor! She is not coming—I swear it.

Raises his hand tragically as STELLA *appears,* L. 1 E. *Both rise quickly.*

(*aside, crosses,* R.) By Jove, I'm trapped.

ELLA. Good evening, Mrs. Lee; you're just in time. (*to* FRED) Let me congratulate you on your success in deception.

FRED (*aside to her*). It's all a mistake—don't make a scene.

STEL. I really beg pardon for this intrusion.

ELLA. Oh, Mrs. Lee, don't apologize—I am the only intruder here. I am glad you have come—Mr. Town was growing quite impatient. It's a lovely evening for a tete-a-tete ; and, now that you are here, he may be able to keep awake. With your permission, Mrs. Lee. (*bows, crosses,* L.—*aside*) I'd like to pinch her and shake him. It's an awful shame ; but what better can you expect from a man ! [*Exit,* L. 1 E.

STEL. What is the matter—have I done anything wrong ?

FRED. Not at all. You only happened to come here at a very awkward moment, and seemed to give me the lie.

STEL. I don't understand you.

FRED. It's all owing to my stupid desire to teaze. Ella and I have had a little misunderstanding, and, in return for her snubbing me, I told her that I was expecting you, and at the very moment I was explaining the joke—presto—you appeared.

STEL. She will believe now my coming here was preconcerted.

FRED. I fear I'll have some trouble to make her believe otherwise.

STEL. I can hardly thank you for this, Mr. Town. (*crosses,* R.)

FRED. Now, for Heaven sake, don't you get angry. I'm always blundering into some scrape. Of course I had no idea you would come out here.

STEL. (*sits,* R.). You have probably placed another obstacle in my path. In her jealousy she may compromise my position here.

FRED. I m the only one will suffer ; she's too proud to say anything about it. But what brought you out here—is anything the matter ?

STEL. No—I could not stay in the house—the air seemed to stifle me ; I wanted to be alone.

FRED. He has come.

STEL. I know it.

FRED. Did he see you ?

STEL. No. He is going back to town to-morrow—I heard his father tell Ella so.

FRED. It's a wonder he stays over night. Home's the last place to look for him. Still, if you stay here, you must meet.

STEL. I presume so.

FRED. Then what will you do ?

STEL. I don't know.

FRED. Well, by Jove, this is the strangest thing I ever heard of in all my life.

STEL. Life is made up of incongruities. Out of many a wild chimera has sprung permanent results. The fact that a thing is strange is no guarantee of its being impossible.

FRED. Well, hang me if I can understand it. You insisted upon coming here—but I don't see what good can come of it. Of course you have some plan.

STEL. (*rises*). My main resolve has been the determination not tamely to submit to a flagrant wrong. I will not silently accept this man's dismissal—that would be to share his sin. (*crosses*, L.)

FRED (R. C.). But have you no settled plan ?

STEL. (L. C.). I had two—one has already failed.

FRED. Failed!

STEL. Yes. I came here first to see this Miss Adair, the woman to whom Mr. Randall would give his son, *my husband*. (FRED *starts*) There —I know what I say. Do you think I will admit, even to myself, that I have no just claim upon this man ? I may be his victim, but I have never been his accomplice. I had hoped to tell this woman frankly the truth, and trust to her woman nature to aid me. I have seen her, and she is not the woman for my confession. She would not pity me—I could not confide in her.

FRED. That is natural.

STEL. It is not jealousy ; I don't like her. You know we women don't stop to reason ; we jump to conclusions. I don't like this Miss Adair— I can't understand myself—I don't know what is actuating me, but I believe that my way to success *crosses the track of her past life.*

FRED. Why, what do you mean ? her past is well-known.

STEL. I don't know. You have promised to help me ; see if you cannot find a clue to something. She may have a secret. I know this sounds foolish. I may believe there is something because I hope for it ; but remember I am a poor, lone woman struggling with fate, and I must hope.

FRED. I will do all in my power to aid you, on my honor. I never liked this Miss Adair, but still I believe you wrong her. What was your other plan ?

STEL. To see Ralph alone, and trust Heaven for the result. But I must not hurry—I must watch my time—failure there would be death. And now—there is another danger. •

FRED. What is it ?

STEL. Miss Prim is here ; the lady you saw leaving my cottage.

FRED. The deuce.

STEL. She is visiting Mrs. Malvernon.

FRED. Why, confound it, that's where I live ; Mrs. Malvernon is my aunt by marriage. I wonder if she'll know me.

STEL. She will know me. Should she see me I will be forced to leave here. Miss Adair dislikes me as it is.

FRED. Well, I swear, this is too bad. Hadn't I better see her, and explain something ?

STEL. Ah, you do not know her. My only hope will be in seeing her alone, and try to persuade her to be silent.

FRED (*crosses*, L.). Hello—by Jove, they're coming.

STEL. Who ?

FRED. Look. (*points* L.)

STEL. Ralph—and with her.

FRED. They mustn't see us here—come.

Music. He leads her up—they conceal themselves by boat house. RALPH *and* CORA *enter*, L. 1 E.

RALPH (R.). ⊥ am sorry at least that you decline to listen.

CORA (L.). I decline for both our sakes. I have nothing of the romantic in my nature, Mr. Randall. Life has taught me to be practical. As I do not elevate you to the position of a god in the present, I will not trouble myself to inquire if you have been a hero in the past.

RALPH (*seriously*). But suppose I have been a devil?

CORA. Oh, Mr. Randall! I am not absurd enough to imagine anything so melo-dramatic. I know the young men of the present day are a little wild, but you know I am not puritanical. I don't like prosaic men.

RALPH. If you will let me make a full confession.

CORA. I am really proud of the confidence you have in me; but, as I cannot give you absolution, I must decline to act as father confessor. (*crosses* R)

RALPH (*sadly*). You are right, Miss Adair—you cannot give me absotion

CORA (*turns to him*). Well, come then, let us drop this subject forever. I have neither the intention nor desire to pry into your secrets. Let us roll a stone against the tomb of the past, and place a seal upon it forever. (*turns away, sits* R)

RALPH. I cannot, of course. force this upon you; I wish to be frank and honest with you—you decline to hear me; you will be good enough to remember this in the future and acquit me, at least, of intentional deception.

CORA. Well, Mr. Randall, if I was of a suspicious nature, I might be induced, from your manner, to believe you a villain, I prefer, however, with your permission to regard you as a gentleman.

RALPH (*aside*). If she selected her words with a knowledge of the truth, she could not wound me more. (*aloud*) My object in seeking to make a confession, was that you might judge for yourself to which of the titles you mention I have the best claim. I will come now to the main object. You are aware of my father's wishes?

CORA. As of my own parents' desire.

RALPH. It seems that we have both been used as puppets in this matter; but it is too late to speak of that now I am given to understand that you consent to the arrangement.

CORA. My poor father's wish was always a command to me, and since I have been here I have learned to obey your father almost as implicitly.

RALPH. Although you are well prepared, Miss Adair, for the proposal I am about to make, I will yet strive to be candid. I will not speak of love. We have seen so little of each other that any attempt on my part to make this an affair of the heart would be absurd.

CORA (*rises*). I have none of the school-girl's enthusiasm, Mr. Randall, and, if I have little of romance in my nature, I have still less of sentiment. I perfectly agree with you as to the absence of love in this matter. The engagement in which we are entangled is the work of our parents. and is only binding upon us in so far as we deem their wishes worthy of respect.

RALPH. I am glad that you are prepared to look upon this in a practical light. The past has left some marks upon my heart that I find it difficult to obliterate, and I am candid enough to acknowledge that my father's wishes alone would not be sufficient to influence my conduct; if, however, you are willing to accept so imperfect a suitor, I will seal this paternal engagement by offering you my hand. (STELLA *staggers, clings to* FRED *for support.*)

CORA. Accustomed from my childhood to regard you as my future husband, and remembering my promise to my dead father, I have no course open to me—but to accept.

RALPH. We accept the engagement, then—which I believe we understand to be a union of hands but not of hearts. (*turns away.*)

CORA (*aside*). I knew my man, and I have won. (*sits, R.*)

RALPH (L., *at chair, aside*). I have done it—saved my inheritance at the sacrifice of my honor.

FRED (*at back*, L., *to* STELLA). Do you hear?

STEL. (*calmly*). Hush. *Watch, but wait.*

Picture—CURTAIN.

ACT III.

SCENE.—*Drawing-room in* RANDALL'S *villa.*

Discovery.—ELLA *and* EOLA *play duet as curtain rises ;* MISS PRIM *on sofa,* L. ; CORA *seated on ottoman*, C ; MRS. MALVERNON *stands at piano.*

MRS. M. (*after duet*). Thank you, my dears ; that was perfectly ruining.

CORA. Are you fond of music, Miss Prim ?

PRIM. I'm fond of church music and some sacred songs, but I don't like those double pieces ; they make too much noise.

CORA. That is often a trouble with duets.

PRIM. What's that piece called ?

CORA. I really must plead ignorance. Ella.

ELLA. Yes. (*comes down.*)

CORA. Miss Prim would like to know the name of the duet you just finished. (*goes up to window.*)

ELLA (*crosses to sofa*). It's called——. It's perfectly lovely, isn't it ?

PRIM. No ; I don't like it. Can you play "When Dropping Tears Refresh my Soul ?"

ELLA. I never heard of that piece ; what is it—a polka ?

PRIM. It's a hymn ; we sing it in Dorcas.

MRS. M. (*comes down*, R., *with* EOLA). You must be mistaken.

EOLA. No, I'm not ; ask Ella. (CORA *sits at piano, turns music.*)

MRS. M. Come, talk to my sister, and I will. (*they go* C.) Matilda, this young lady wants to talk to you about Dorcas. When she returns to Chicago she wants to give them the benefit of your opinion.

PRIM. Gracious! haven't you a Dorcas society out there ?

EOLA. Yes, I suppose—really I don't know ?

PRIM. Well, did I ever! Why, Chicago must be worse than New York. You've got churches, haven't you ?

EOLA. Oh, yes. (*sits on sofa beside* PRIM. MRS. MALVERNON, *having drawn* ELLA *away, stands talking to her*, R. H.)

PRIM. Have you got a Young Men's Christian Association ?

EOLA. I suppose so, but my papa don't like me to know much about young men.

PRIM. Very proper, my dear ; very proper. Young men of the present day are very wicked, but when they belong to the Young Men's Christian Association, they become the spiritual guides of the weaker sex.

MRS. M. (R. C.). You're a foolish, silly child. I know my nephew better than yon, and I say it's all nonsense. Fred loves you as well as ever.

ELLA (*sits* L. *of table*, R.). Does he ? Well, he takes a strange way of showing it.

MRS. M. Why, you don't expect him to be kneeling at your feet all the time, do you ? (EOLA *and* PRIM *go up, look at picture on easel.*)

ELLA. Yes, sooner than have him at the feet of another woman. What's the use of being engaged to a man if you don't get all his attentions ?

MRS. M. Why, you unreasonable little dunce ! You surely don't think Fred cares for Mrs. Lee ?

ELLA. I don't know. You never can tell what men care for; they're worse than a Chinese puzzle.

MRS. M. Well, now take care. Any puzzle can be solved if you take time enough. Now, no man ought to be a puzzle to a woman. They're shrewd enough in business, but bless you, they're perfect babies in love.

ELLA. And, like babies, throw away an old toy when they see the glitter of a new one

MRS. M. The man who is led by his eye alone may do so; the man who is led by his heart, never. Now, Fred loves you.

ELLA. Oh, pshaw !

MRS. M. There, don't jump ; I know what I say. A man, even in love, requires very delicate handling. You may gently wind him around your finger; but one harsh twist—one turn too much, and you find your finger cut and your slave fled. Now, I know Fred's nature better than you do; but I fear he has got himself in a scrape.

ELLA (*quickly*). What is it ?

MRS. M. I'm not certain yet. Now where did Fred tell you he was going when he left here ?

ELLA. To New York, to sketch animals in Central Park.

MRS. M. So he told me ; but he was really down in New Jersey.

ELLA. How do you know ?

MRS M. My sister recognized him as soon as he came in—spoke of meeting him in Jersey, and the way Fred stammered a reply, showed he had a secret.

ELLA. A secret ! Put it in the plural, Mrs. Malvernon; that young man is above having only one secret. (*rises, crosses* C. MRS. MALVERNON *stops her.*)

MRS. M. I think I have an idea what this secret is about. Don't do anything hasty. Keep this young man in leading strings, and trust me.

ALBERY SEDLEY *enters*, D. L.

ELLA. Oh, Mr. Sedley, you're just in time to save us ladies from ennui.

SEDLEY. Charmed, really. (*bows to* EOLA)

MRS. M. (*aside*) Just like a girl—she'll spoil all now by flirting with that dunce. (*goes to* CORA, *at piano.*)

ELLA. (R C.). I want to introduce you to Mrs. Malvernon's sister. (*crosses* L. C.) Miss Prim, let me make you acquainted with a friend of mine, Mr. Albery Sedley.

PRIM. (*comes down* L). Sedley—Sedley. Any relation to Dick Sedley ?

SED He's my father. (EOLA *stands back of sofa.*)

PRIM. Well, I declare ! Why I knew your father when I was a child.

He used to live near us in Jersey, and supplied Long Branch with ice.
(*sits on sofa.*)

SED. (*shocked*). By Jove, madam, it's a mistake! it wasn't my father.
(*goes* R., *looks over books on table.*)

ELLA. Oh, you're mistaken, Miss Prim; his father's a lawyer.

PRIM. Yes, it's the same—he made a fortune in ice and came to New York, and set up in the law

ELLA. Well, have it so. His father is immensely rich, and the son is a very proper young man.

PRIM. I don't like him—he parts his hair in the middle.

ELLA. He's a member of the Young Men's Christian Association.
(*goes* R., *to* SEDLEY.)

PRIM (*to* EOLA). Do you know him?

EOLA. Yes; and he's a very nice young man.

PRIM. Humph! What's your father think of him?

EOLA. Oh, papa's not a judge of young men.

ELLA. (*to* SEDLEY). I know—you expected a *tete-a-tete*.

SED. Well—I thought——

ELLA. Of course. I'll fix it. (*crosses* c.) Eola, Mr. Sedley would like to take a stroll in the park.

EOLA (*rises*). Are you going?

ELLA. Yes. Will you join us, Miss Prim?

PRIM. No; I don't care to walk unless I have something to do.

SED. (*aside*). By Jove, I think walking is having something to do.
(*offers arm*)

CORA (*rises from piano*). Are you going out?

ELLA (*going*). Just for a moment; we'll be back soon.
[*Exeunt* ELLA, EOLA *and* SEDLEY, *at window.*

MRS M. (*comes down* R.). There, Miss Adair, you see what that young torment is about? She's getting up a flirtation between that innocent Eola and Mr. Sedley.

CORA It is an act in perfect keeping with Ella's usual thoughtlessness.

MRS. M. That's her object. Oh, I can read young girls, my dear, without spectacles, if I am an old woman. She'll make an excuse and leave them together, and if Mr Wimberly should see them, then the little Eola would suffer. (*crosses* c.) Come, Matilda; are you ready?

PRIM (*rises*). Ready! Certainly.

MRS. M (c.. *to* CORA). I would like to ask you one favor. Fred and Ella are trying to get up a quarrel. Now, as you are constantly with her, will you try and make her reasonable?

PRIM (L.). She's too headstrong to manage.

CORA (R.). You are right; still I will do my best.

MRS. M. Thank you. Come, Matilda.

As they go, STELLA *enters* D. R. PRIM *starts.*

STEL. Miss Adair, I—(*sees* PRIM, *starts violently—turns away agitated.*)

PRIM. Gracious! You here?

CORA (*surprised*). Why, do you know Mrs. Lee, Miss Prim?

PRIM. No, I don't know Mrs. Lee—but I know——

STEL. (*with sudden resolve, crosses to her*). Pray pardon me, Miss Prim, your presence here somewhat surprised me. (*aside to her, quickly*) Don't say a word till I see you again; if you speak you will ruin me.

CORA. I scarcely understand you, Miss Prim.

STEL. (*tries to be calm*). This lady is acquainted with a secret of mine; may I ask you to let it remain such?

CORA. Excuse me, I was addressing Miss Prim. She will certainly agree with me that I am justified in demanding an explanation.

PRIM. Yes—certainly.

CORA. Then, Miss Prim, if this person is not Mrs. Lee, who is she? (*pause—STELLA looks at PRIM imploringly.*)

PRIM. I won't answer that question—I don't know why she is here, but I will say no more.

STEL. (*aside to her*). God bless you! (*crosses to fire.*)

CORA. Then I have simply to regret your determination.

PRIM (*to STELLA*). I don't understand this, and I don't like it. I hope you'll be able to explain. Come, sister. (*goes D. L.*)

MRS. M. I regret, Miss Adair, my sister's refusal to explain.

CORA. It does not matter; it will scarcely affect the result.

MRS. M. You'll run over soon?

CORA (*goes to door with them*). To-morrow perhaps.

MRS. M. Till then. [*Bows and exits, D. L., with PRIM.*

CORA (*comes down slowly, C.*). Now, then, madam, I am ready for your explanation.

STEL. Please don't ask me now.

CORA. By what name shall I address you in future?

STEL. It is hardly necessary to ask that question.

CORA. You are evidently here under an assumed name; and there is only one construction to put upon that.

STEL. What do you mean?

CORA. I mean that you either have no right to a husband's name, or feel ashamed of your own.

STEL. (*advances angrily*). Why, do you dare—(*draws back*) I beg your pardon, I forgot myself.

FRED *appears in window, C.*

CORA. I must request you to keep your temper, madam, or *miss*—I am somewhat uncertain how to call you.

STEL. I have given you the name of Mrs. Lee. The fact that I have a secret is scarcely sufficient reason for subjecting me to insult. Being of your sex should entitle me to some consideration; but you hated me from the first.

CORA. Oh, pardon me. My hatred, like my friendship, is confined to a circle somewhat above your own. But I will tell you this——

FRED. Look out, there's some one here.

CORA (*starts, goes R.*). Listening, Mr. Town?

FRED (*comes down*). All the fault of my artist nature, Miss Adair. I was studying character. The light and shade were perfect, and the humble demeanor of the dependent contrasted very well with the courtesy of the high-born lady.

CORA. I am glad the scene afforded you so much pleasure. It will make a fine companion picture to a certain tete-a-tete in the park.

FRED. I will be charmed to utilize the subject if you will explain it more fully.

CORA. I would not presume to give a spur to your genius, but, as a hint to your imagination, let me suggest that in a moonlight promenade there are often more listeners—*than the stars.* [*Exit, D. R.*

STEL. (*comes to FRED*). Ella has told her of our meeting in the park.

FRED (*crosses to fire, annoyed*). I thought Ella was above that. What has this Miss Adair discovered?

STEL. Miss Prim has seen me, and though—Heaven bless her—she refused to speak, there was enough said to show I was not Mrs. Lee.

FRED. By Jove, I wish this dear Miss Prim had never left the obscurity of Jersey. You'll have to leave here.

STEL. I know that. This Miss Adair hates me, and, as she does as she pleases here, my dismissal will not be delayed.

FRED. Since it is sure to come, why wait for it?

STEL. I do not intend to. I will leave this house, but not the neighborhood, until I see him once more face to face. This woman can have no suspicion of the truth, and yet look at her manner towards me; she is coarse—there is a pretence in her refinement—I feel she is not a lady —and then to think of her as his—Oh, Heaven, help me; I cannot bear that—it will kill me. (*sinks sobbing on ottoman,* c. FRED *goes to her.*)

FRED (c.). Come, this won't do. On the path you have taken there is no resting place for tears. Listen to me. You have taken a decided dislike to Miss Adair. I regard that as natural; but I have promised to be your friend, and I will humor even your whims. Now this Miss Adair may have a suspicion of the truth.

STEL. (*startled*). How could she?

FRED. Buddles was spying down in Eatentown—she has a strong influence over him, and he may have told her what he saw. If so she has only to couple Miss Prim's recognition of you with Miss Prim's residence in Jersey to come at a shrewd guess of the truth.

STEL. That is true.

FRED. Now this Buddles came here with this Miss Adair, and, if she really has any secret in her life, Buddles is the man to reveal it.

STEL. (*springs up*). I never thought of that.

FRED. Well, don't think of it again until I know more.

STEL. But you will try?

FRED. On my honor as your friend.

Takes her hand. ELLA *enters at window. They start*—FRED *goes to fire.*

ELLA. I must really beg your pardon. I regret to interrupt you, Mrs. Lee, but my father desires you to have Mr. Randall's room over the library in readiness. My brother returns to-day for some time. (*sits at piano.*)

STEL. I will attend to it at once. (*aside, going* R.) She believes I am trying to win her lover; if she knew the truth, would she despise or pity me? [*Exit,* D. R.

FRED. Ella.

ELLA (*playing*). What is it?

FRED. I wish you'd stop that noise and come here.

ELLA. Thank you—I prefer to stay where I am.

FRED. Well, then, I must come to you. (*goes up.*)

ELLA. Don't trouble yourself.

FRED (*leans over her*). Ella, I wish to speak to you very seriously.

ELLA. Now go away, Fred Town, and leave me alone. (*rises, crosses to sofa.*)

FRED (*goes to her*). Will you please to remain in one place, and listen to me?

ELLA (*sits on sofa.*) No, I won't; I won't listen to a word you say. (*covers her ears with her hands.*)

FRED. Come, now, be reasonable. You don't understand this.

ELLA. I can't hear a word you say.

FRED. You can't?

ELLA. No.

FRED. Now, don't be silly. You think you have cause to be angry, don't you? Well, you haven't. Do you think I'd deceive you, eh?

Won't you answer me? You don't suppose I care for Mrs. Lee, do you? Eh! She's a very pretty woman though, isn't she? (ELLA *makes a slight movement*) Has such a sweet and winning way, hasn't she? And then her disposit.on—she's very amiable, isn't she?

ELLA (*springs up angrily*). Fred Town, you're a brute! (*crosses*, R.)

FRED. Oh, no—just at present I'm a doctor, applying a severe remedy in order to restore your hearing. I shouldn't like to have a deaf wife.

ELLA. Oh, so you expect to marry me?

FRED. Of course—it's all settled isn t it?

ELLA. Well, it's agreed on, but not settled. From what I've seen of mankind, I'd never believe I had a husband until the ring was on my finger and the marriage certificate was in my pocket; and men are such slippery individuals, I'd scarcely be sure of it then.

FRED. You have a poor opinion of our sex.

ELLA. Of course I have; so has every woman of experience.

FRED. Yet, in stigmatizing our sex you cast a reflection upon your own.

ELLA. How so?

FRED. How can man be all evil since perfect woman sprang from his rib?

ELLA. Easy enough. All that was good of him left with his rib—all that was evil remained.

FRED. It is probably, then, upon the principle that like objects repel, that this perfect woman is so partial to this imperfect man. Still it is to be regretted that even perfect woman sometimes stoops to unworthy acts.

ELLA. Do you refer to me?

FRED. I regret to say I do.

ELLA. And I have done something, then, even more silly than listening to your vows?

FRED. You have condescended to act the part of tale-bearer.

ELLA. If you refer to what took place in the park the other evening, it is false. I mentioned it to no one

FRED. What! You didn't?

ELLA. No.

FRED (*aside*). Made another blunder, by Jove!

ELLA. I'm glad to know your true opinion of me, Mr. Town.

FRED. I beg your pardon, Ella. It was all a mistake.

ELLA. Don't speak to me. I hate you! (*goes R.*)

FRED. Yes—but, Ella——

ELLA. Silence, scorpion! [*Exit, angrily*, L. D.

FRED (R.). Well, I'd better turn Don Quixote at once. I think I'd come out better in a struggle with a windmill than in a contest with a woman. Confound this business! it's getting me into a nice scrape.

SEDLEY *enters, moodily, from the park.*

SED. (*comes down*, C., *absently*). Hello, Fred.

FRED (*savagely*). Hello.

SED. (*surprised*). Why, what's the matter?

FRED (*abruptly*). Matter! what do you see the matter? What makes you ask such stupid questions? (*goes up.*)

SED. (*dolefully*). Don't be angry, old fellow; I'm awfully blue.

FRED (*turns quickly*). You are? Give me your hand. (*shakes*) I'm very sorry to hear it. (*aside*) Strange how you can feel for a fellow when you have the same complaint.

SED. (*takes out note-book*). I've got something father gave me for you—I believe it's a check. (*gives envelope.*)

FRED. For me ! (*opens it, takes out paper.*)

SED. Yes ; he's delighted with the picture.

FRED. By Jove ! (*drops envelope.*)

SED. (*picks up envelope*). What's wrong ? (*reads envelope*) Why, hang it, I've given you the wrong one. Why, what the deuce have I done with the one father gave me ? (*looks in his book.*)

FRED. Where did you get this.

SED. Found it in the park. I suppose it fell from Miss Adair's desk. Here's her name on the envelope. (*gives envelope.*)

FRED. Have you read it ?

SED. No—I never read unless I have to; it's too much trouble. What is it ?

FRED. Only some accounts. I'll give it to her. (*aside, crosses,* L.) When it has served my purpose. (*aloud*) By the way, what gave you the blues ?

SED. Mr. Wimberly—he saw me walking with his daughter in the park—took her under his arm, and shook me. Now, that's what I call small.

FRED. Look out.

- WIMBERLY *and* EOLA *enter at window.*

Ah, my dear sir, we were just speaking of you. Good morning, Miss Eola ; what can I do to serve you ?

EOLA (c.). Get papa in a good humor—he's so cross.

WIM. (L. c). Tut, tut, Miss ; what are you saying?

EOLA. Well, it's true ; you're scolding me all the time. (*go up.*)

WIM. (*to* FRED). Hear that ? That's a plump contradiction from my own child. Well, if I stay here much longer, no one will ever believe she was brought up in the innocence of Chicago. (*sits on sofa.* SEDLEY *looks carefully at* WIMBERLY, *gradually goes to* EOLA, *who sits at piano.*)

FRED (*back to fire*). That is not very complimentary to our girls.

WIM. Truth seldom is. You don't bring up girls right here. They study matrimony in their babyhood by having a toy beau for their toy doll, and graduate from the nursery with a full appreciation of the verb to love.

FRED. It's our national character to dislike leading-strings. Everything is fast here, so we soon jump out of childhood.

WIM. Stuff, sir, stuff. Childhood is the time for preparation ; and if our parents would only keep us out of our first boots a little longer, we wouldn't be in such danger of butting our brains out in a struggle with the world. It's no use talking, sir ; we're too fast, much too fast.

FRED You're rather severe on your own country.

WIM. Who has a better right, sir ? What's the good of being an American if you can't express your opinion ! But, bless me, we're going ahead so fast it's getting dangerous now to do that. Still I don't like your great city, and I say so.

FRED. Not like New York ? That's strange. The Frenchmen tell us to "see Paris, and die ; ' now we say here, see New York, and live.

WIM. Live ' Why, confound it, a man can't live here without he has a fortune, and then he has a powder magazine. To live in New York, my young friend, a man must be rich ; but if a man wants to be safe in New York he must be poor ; and even then he shouldn't ride in the horse cars after dark.

FRED. You seem to have studied our city.

Wim. I have. I read the newspapers, and a man who does that, sir, is not easily deceived. Now just look at your streets in winter ; a heavy fall of snow is an excuse for the contractors, and a sudden thaw a stimulant to the doctors; and then your police force—bless me, just think of it—you give one man a beat of four or five miles, and then curse the poor devil if he's at one end when a row's going on at the other.

Fred. Oh, we intend to remedy all that. We expect to put in an entire reform party next election.

Wim. And that will have just as much effect as trying to reform one rogue by knocking him down with another rogue. The reform you want is to reform the politicians themselves, and, damme, that's difficult. We've tried it in Chicago, and found out.

Fred Well, we must look to the new school of philosophy for rescue. They're making rapid strides.

Wim. There, that'll do ; I don't like those new-fangled ideas.

Fred. Have you studied them ?

Wim. Yes, sir ; and I've bothered my old head over the Development Theory, Natural Selection and Evolution, and I consider it—all bosh.

Fred (laughing). You don't believe in the origin of man, then, according to Darwin !

Wim. No, sir, emphatically no, sir. Do you suppose I could take any pleasure in reading over my geneological record if I thought an ape was grinning at me over the top ?

Fred. The presence of the ape would not affect your bank account.

Wim. The man who has no pride, sir, beyond his bank account, is only worthy to be the descendant of brutes.

Fred. So you're not very partial to philosophy ?

Wim. All I ask of philosophy, sir, is to teach me how to live without bothering my head as to why I live. (starts—looks suddenly around—sees Eola and Sedley.)

Fred (quickly). As you say, philosophy is——

Wim. (rises). Hang philosophy. You young rascal, you've made me forget that party. Eola !

Eola (rises, runs down, c). Yes, papa. Just look what Mr. Sedley gave me. Isn't it good ? (gives card photograph).

Wim. (looks at it). Pshaw ! What do you want with his picture ? he isn't dead.

Eola. To put in my album. Ella gave me two beauties. One's my sensation album, and I have it half full of celebrated criminals already ; the other's my choice one—that's the only picture I have for that.

Wim. Humph ! This is very choice. (crosses, R.) Come, I want you.

Eola. Right away, papa ?

Wim. (at door, R.) Yes, miss. I want to see that sensation album.

Eola (to Sedley, who stands up, L.). I'm very much obliged to you, Mr. Sedley ; such a good picture.

Wim. Eola ! (she crosses —exits, quickly, D. R.) Excuse me, sir. (aside) Parts his hair in the middle. Bah ! [Exit, D. R.

Sed. (pause—comes c.). He don't like me.

Fred (comes c.). No, he don't seem very partial. I did what I could.

Sed. I'm much obliged to you, old fellow. She has my picture— that's something. But come, we're out in the cold—let's go. (goes L. D.)

Fred. Well, I suppose that's about the best thing I can do.

Goes up as Buddles *enters,* D. R., *with receipt-book.*

(aside) Just the man. (aloud) I won't go just yet, Sedley.

Sed. Shall I wait ?

FRED. Oh, no. (SEDLEY *exits*, D. L.) Busy, Mr. Buddles?

BUD. (*opens desk down* R.). Always busy, sir—business is what I live on. Just been collecting rent. (*makes note in book.*)

FRED. Pleasant amusement? (*lounges on sofa.*)

BUD When they haven't got the money, yes, sir; when they have got it—no, sir.

FRED. How's that?

BUD. When they have the money it's tame, when they haven't got it —it's exciting. (*closes desk.*)

FRED. You like excitement then?

BUD. Yes, sir, keeps down my flesh.

FRED. Well, if no one interrupts us, I think I can give you a little excitement. But first one th ng—When I returned here I requested you to blot something from your memory.

BUD. (C.). And you gave me the blotter.

FRED. Ten dollars.

BUD. And I forgot I ever saw Mrs. Lee, as I'm an honest man.

FRED. If some one had offered double the money, it might have restored your memory.

BUD. No, sir; I'd have asked you for another blotter.

FRED. I see you appreciate the value of money.

BUD. I do, as I'm an honest man.

FRED. Well, how much did Miss Adair give you for the information that I met Mrs. Lee in the park the other evening?

BUD. Not a penny.

FRED. Then it was you who told her?

BUD. It was, as I'm an honest man.

FRED. Well, you're candid.

BUD. My weakness, sir—I never tell a lie to a patron.

FRED. Thank you, you do me too much honor. But now that we are on the subject, I suppose it was the same lady who sent you spying down in Jersey.

BUD. It was, as I'm an honest man.

FRED. And what did the lady pay for that?

BUD. Not a copper.

FRED (*aside*). On the right track, by Jove. (*aloud*) Sit down.

BUD. Sit down?

FRED (*points to chair at fire*). Take a seat there—I want to patronize you. I couldn't think of letting such an honest man stand.

BUD. (*sits timidly by fire*). Don't joke, sir, it makes me nervous.

FRED. Ah, my dear Buddles, now we're comfortable. So it seems you don't charge this Miss Adair anything?

BUD. (*savagely*). I would if I could, but I can't.

FRED. Why not?

BUD. Because—(*stops suddenly*) Because I can't.

FRED. That answer is somewhat indefinite, my dear Buddles. Now I suppose you are aware that this Miss Adair does not like me?

BUD. She hates you.

FRED. Well I did not wish to accuse a lady of such a vulgar animosity as hate. You are more candid if less polite.

BUD. I like to be plain.

FRED. Well, you can afford to be plain in speech, for you're by no means plain in person.

BUD. Well I don't pretend to be a handsome man.

FRED. Well, no, Buddles, you're not exactly handsome, but there is something out of the common about you, an originality, a strong individuality; but to the point. Miss Adair don't like me; granted; I don't like her; acknowledged. Now, when a person hates another, what's the usual course?

BUD. Stab 'em in the back, as I'm an honest man.

FRED. Well—hem—you put it most too strong, my dear Buddles.

BUD. I don't mean physically stick—but theoretically stick. Trip 'em up; spoil their game.

FRED. Then you think there is a game?

BUD. (*frightened*). Oh—I don't know.

FRED. The blotter has been applied to your memory, I see. I must try and find a chemical restorative Now you give your services to this lady gratis, and as you are so fond of money, I can only account for that in one way, viz.. *that she holds you in her power.*

BUD. (*starts up*). What!

FRED. Sit still, my dear Buddles, it'll grow exciting soon.

BUD. It's exciting now, as I'm an honest man. (*sits.*)

FRED. Now you were in the service of Miss Adair's father, and came to this country with her; ergo—you must be well posted as to her history.

BUD. Excuse me—I—I must go. (*rises timidly.*)

FRED. Now. my dear Buddles, do sit still—you make me nervous jumping up in that way.

BUD. (*aside*). He's drunk, he must be drunk. (*sits.*)

FRED. Now there is no use in my questioning the lady herself, so I must look to you for information; but in order to be equal with Miss Adair; I must, like her, *hold you in my power.*

BUD. (*rises*). Excuse me—I—I can't stand it—the fire's too warm. (*crosses,* C.)

FRED (*takes out the paper*). You'll find it warmer in a prison.

BUD. (*with back to him*). A prison!

FRED To the cell of which I hold the key.

BUD. (*turning*). Stop—that's mine.

FRED (*sits up*). Excuse me, there's a higher claimant.

BUD. Who?

FRED (*rises*). The law.

BUD But Miss—she had—how did you get that?

FRED. By accident, my dear Buddles. I appreciated them, retained them, and now utilize them. From this paper I find that you have appropriated some of Mr. Randall's money in a manner known to the law as stealing. Now there are many men calling themselves honest, who steal, but when the law finds them out, they are, I believe, punished as criminals

BUD. When they're poor—yes; and I am poor, sir, but I'm an hon—humble man. Don't show that paper, Mr. Town; I haven't got any political influence, and I'd be sent to prison. I'll do all you want, gratis. I was in her power—now—damn it, now I'm in yours.

FRED (*stands near fire*). You'll help me, then?

BUD. (*close to him*). I will, sir, as I'm an honest man.

RANDALL *and* RALPH *enter,* D. L., BUDDLES *starts, and kneeling quickly rakes fire,* FRED *crosses,* C., *meets* RALPH.

RALPH (*coldly*). Good day, sir. (*goes to fire.*)

RAN. (*goes to desk*) Anything new, Fred?

FRED (C.). I believe not, sir.

RALPH (*to* BUDDLES). What are you doing?

BUD. Raking the fire.

RALPH. Are you cold?

Bud. Yes, sir—fear it's the ague—it commenced with a fever and it ended with a chill. (*puts poker down, goes a little up.*)

Ferd. Mr. Randall, if you can spare Mr. Buddles a short time, I would like to take him to my studio.

Ran. What for? (*sits at desk, writing.*)

Fred. To paint his picture; I am illustrating the Darwin theory, and having evolved as far as the ape, I am now ready to commence on the man.

Ran. And you propose making Buddles the connecting link, eh? Well, take him along.

Fred. Thank you. (*going, aside to* Buddles) Follow me at once.
[*Exit, door* L.

Bud. (*aside*). I'm a connecting link. eh—I think not—for I'll separate some hearts in this house, as I'm an honest man.   [*Exit,* D. L.

Ralph (*on sofa*). I wish you wouldn't keep that fellow, Buddles, here.

Ran. Why not?

Ralph. Because he's treacherous. He has deceit written all over him.

Ran. You can't always judge by appearances; men with the forms of Apollo have yet stooped to deceive.

Ralph. That is true.

Ran. I don't pretend to defend this fellow. I keep him here because he was in the employment of Cora's father, and she is attached to him. But I believe we did not come here to discuss Buddles. (*rises*) Here is the account I promised you; you can read it at your leisure; you will find there all the information you need about the estate. (*crosses, gives paper he has taken from desk.*)

Ralph. I did not ask for the estimate, it was your own proposal. (*takes it.*)

Ran. I am aware of that; but it is my wish for you to have it. You will find there, checked off, such property as I propose conveying to you in trust, as soon as my wishes have been carried out.

Ralph. In trust?

Ran. Yes, sir, in trust; but what comes to you at my death, will be in fee. Now, I understand that you have offered your hand to Cora. (*sits,* R. C.)

Ralph. I see she has hastened to inform you of the fact.

Ran. I requested her to tell me the truth, and she did so. Now, in speaking to her, did you mention the past?

Ralph. You might have asked her that, also.

Ran. I prefer asking you, sir.

Ralph. Well, I attempted a confession, but she poetically requested me to roll a stone against the tomb of the past, and place a seal upon it.

Ran. Very good, the truth has been offered, she cannot accuse us of any deception; but let me suggest to you the propriety of not rolling that stone so tight as to forget the necessities of a certain person who has a claim upon you.

Ralph. What do you mean?

Ran. I mean that before you seal up the past altogether, you should place behind that stone an annuity sufficient to guarantee the future of your child.

Ralph (*annoyed*). We won't speak of that, please.

Ran. It is to speak of that, sir, that I brought you here. I do not wish that the offspring of my son, sir, should be left to starve.

Ralph (*springs up angrily*). I do not intend that he shall starve, sir.

Ran. Very good, but I want this provision made in such a manner, that in the future, there will be no occasion for you to see either the mother or the child. I will not risk the possibility that the lady to whom I offer you, may reproach me, that her husband visits the house of a worth——

RALPH. Stop, sir; I will not hear a word against her, even from you. The hour that makes me the husband of Miss Adair closes that woman's door against me forever. She would scorn me too deeply to ever receive my visits, even if she does not scorn me now.

RAN. That sounds well, but you must permit me to doubt.

RALPH. Well, permit me, father, to suggest to you the propriety of not referring further to an act of which you were partially the cause.

RAN. (starts up). What, sir! Do you dare make me your accomplice ?

RALPH. In a measure—yes. A parent is morally responsible for a child's acts, and when that child is a son, the responsibility falls most heavily on the father. (crosses, R.)

RAN. (L. C.). What do you mean ?

RALPH (R. C.). I mean, sir, that the child brought up in the atmosphere of fashion, surrounded by wealth, taught the ways of the world, without being shown its hollowness; rocked and dandled through college, and launched into life with a full purse, has a right, if he falls, to turn to that parent, and say—"You profited by experience, why did you not warn me of the dangers ahead ? why did you not show me the rocks on which I might be wrecked ?"

RAN. Why, how in the name of Heaven do you make me to blame?

RALPH. From the manner of my education.

RAN. I endeavored to educate you—as a gentleman.

RALPH. That word signifies nothing. The elegant habitue of society is not always a gentleman, nor the humble toiler in poverty always a common man.

RAN. There, I don't want any of that nonsense; I like to deal with *what is*, not with *what ought to be*. (sits on sofa.)

RALPH. I'm coming to that: I have been guilty of an act not only ungentlemanly, but unmanly. I have deceived a gentle, loving woman——

RAN. Who was silly enough——

RALPH. Stop, sir; I am willing to confess my degredation, but I will not hear a word against the woman who has only to blush for having made the acquaintance of your son.

RAN. As it is evidently your intention to wound my pride to the utmost, sir, I must congratulate you on your choice of words. Since you respect this person so highly, how came you to deceive her so basely ?

RALPH. Through you. She was poor and humble, and I feared your pride. I could not come to you, trusting to your love to out-weigh worldly considerations. I knew your nature, and I feared the loss of the wealth you have taught me to worship. From my very youth you have bound me to accept the woman of your choice, or poverty.

RAN. (rises, crosses, R.) I pledged my word to my old friend, Adair, and my word I never break. (sits R.) Still, if you did not wish to yield to my wishes, I presume you could support your wife like other men.

RALPH. How ? I have received a scholarly education; will it be the means of procuring me a trade ? Can Latin or Greek teach me the rules on 'change, or a knowledge of astronomy fit me for a mercantile position ? I do not lack the willingness to work, sir, but the ability.

RAN. There is plenty of work, if you are forced to look for it.

RALPH. And with what credentials ? I have not the physical practice to endure manual labor, and I have no knowledge of the professions. Cast off by you, I am simply a college graduate, standing upon the threshold of a strange life, with a parchment diploma in my hand, from which I cannot derive the slightest practical information as to the manner in which men win bread.

RAN. Why, do you pretend to say there are no openings for young men in this country?

RALPH. No, sir. The openings are ample for those who have been qualified by experience to fill them; or when a father uses his influence for the interests of his son. But a young man, fresh from college, has no such experience; his education has been theoretical, not practical. He stands in relation to business as a child to life; forced to crawl before he can hope to walk. If he has money and influence, his success is assured; if, however, he lacks both, he will find that his A. B. is no "open sesame," and will be compelled to subsist upon a beggarly salary in some business until he can learn enough to make himself practically useful.

RAN. This case does not apply to me. I was not called upon to learn you a trade or place you in business, when I could leave you ample means to live as a gentleman.

RALPH. But when you make my obedience to your every whim the tenure upon which I hold my claims to your indulgence, you force me into the very deception of which you complain. I deny your right, sir, to educate me for a position in which I am called upon to thank you for my exemption from work, when you claim the privilege of casting me off with the sneer—go and work. I confess I should have preferred a trade in my youth; that would have made me more independent in my manhood.

RAN. (rises). I did not ask you to come home to insult me, sir. I disclaim any connection with your unworthy acts, either directly or indirectly. I have never deceived you in this matter. I gave you frankly to understand that I had pledged my word as to your future, and told you frankly what you must expect if you refused to second it. (crosses. L.)

RALPH. I do not complain of any want of candor on your part, I only question your moral right to force me into a union in which there is no heart.

RAN. I force you into nothing, sir—I simply decline to have my money squandered on an unworthy object, and make certain conditions upon which you shall be my heir. I have a right to make such disposition of my property as pleases me, and, if you decline the conditions, I will leave everything to Ella and Miss Adair, and you will be free to face the world, but without a penny from me to help you on the way.

[Exits, D. L.

RALPH. He is absolutely heartless. Oh, how I despise myself for hesitating. I know what I should do; there is but one honest course open to me—and yet I pause. I have not the courage to do right. I cannot bear that my inheritance should go to a stranger; and yet the more I think upon this marriage the more repulsive it becomes.

ELLA enters, D. R.

ELLA. Why, Ralph. Oh, I'm so glad you're here. Where's papa?

RALPH (L. C). Gone out.

ELLA. I'm glad of that—I want to talk to you alone. I've got something awful to tell you.

RALPH. Oh, not now.

ELLA. Why, what's the matter?

RALPH (going). Nothing—don't bother me. (turns back) There, I didn't mean that, Ella—I'm a little annoyed. I'll just take a stroll in the park a moment; then I'll come and listen patiently; a little fresh air will set me all right. (*aside, going*) God bless her—I'll try and keep the truth from her. [*Exit*, c.

ELLA (*sits on ottoman*, c.). Well, I believe every one is going mad here. One thing is certain, there's something going on that I know nothing about. It's too bad. I hate secrets. If I could only hold Mr. Town tight with one hand, and pinch him with the other, I think I'd feel better.

STELLA *appears, door,* L.

I always had a poor opinion of men, but I did thought Fred—I mean Mr. Town—was an exception. But that's always the way; every girl thinks she has an exception.

STEL. (*comes slowly to her*). Miss Randall.

ELLA (*looks up haughtily*). Are you speaking to me, madam?

STEL. (*sadly*). Yes. I am going to leave here—I am going away forever. I know that none of you will be sorry—I have made many enemies in my brief stay—but I at least wish you to think well of me.

ELLA. I don't pretend to be of any consequence here.

STEL. You have misjudged me, Miss Randall. If I could only tell you all, you would see how I could not wrong you even in thought. I have had great trouble, and Mr. Town has simply acted the part of a noble gentleman towards a lone woman in distress.

ELLA. And even extends his kindness to correspondence.

STEL. I don't understand you, Miss Randall.

ELLA (*rises*). Mr. Buddles brought a letter from Mr. Town. I promised to deliver it—there it is. (*gives letter she has held in her hand*) Now, having assisted in the conveyance of Mr. Town's thoughts I'll leave you to peruse them at your leisure. (*going.*)

STEL. A letter! (*looks at letter surprised; goes down* L.)

ELLA. If you will condescend to take my advice, you will place it with the others you have no doubt received from the same source, tie them with white ribbon, and you'll find them all in good order when your turn comes to send them back. [*Exit*, D. R. *Music, pp.*

STEL. (*sits on sofa*). A letter to me, from Mr. Town! What can it mean? (*opens it nervously - reads*) "Mrs. Lee.—Courage and hope. I've taken the first step on the path you set before me, and expect to achieve more than your most sanguine hopes. The canvass is on the easel, the brush is in my hand, Buddles supplies the colors, and the painted result will astonish no one more than yourself. It is a full moon to-night. If you would like to know the subject of my picture, take a walk in the park, and this time I will take care there are no listeners—*but the stars.* Fred Town." (*rises*) He has made some discovery. Oh, can it be possible that what has seemed a wild fancy, a mad chimera, may yet become a reality? But what good can it do me now. I must leave here or she will force me to go. I will not wait for——(*looks in glass, sees* RALPH *entering* c. *from park*) He here!—face to face at last. (*stands looking in fire, with back to* c.)

RALPH, *entering* c., *comes down.*

RALPH (*looks at her carelessly*). Mrs. Lee, I presume. Don't let me disturb you, madam. (*goes to desk*) I came in expecting to find my sister; I presume she became tired of waiting. (*opens desk, sits.*)

STEL. (*in strange voice*). She has just left.

RALPH. (*writing*). I am not surprised; she seldom remains in one place long.

STEL. Have you any commands, sir ?

RALPH Well, I would like you to have my room well aired, please. It has been so long since I occupied it I suppose it is rather musty.

STEL. I have already attended to it, sir.

RALPH. Thank you—then that is all.

STEL. (*hesitates, then slowly turns, goes* L. C., *faces him*). Have I your permission to retire, sir ?

RALPH. Permission, my dear madam ? Why, I——(*leans back in chair, pen in hand, sees her—springs up*) Great heavens ! Stella !

STEL. I am called here Mrs. Lee, sir.

RALPH. Why, what are you doing here under a false name ?

STEL. Following your example. Gordon was not your real name.

RALPH. Come with me—they mustn't see you here.

STEL. Excuse me, a housekeeper is not confined to one room.

RALPH. What ! You a housekeeper in my father's house !

STEL. Why not ?

RALPH. Why not ? Great Heaven ! you should not have come here.

STEL. If you know anything against my good name, sir; if you can point to any act of *mine* that should bar me from earning my bread in an honest manner, reveal it to your father and he will turn me from the house.

RALPH. Earning your bread ? Why, I left you ample means.

STEL. Did you not know me better than to believe I would touch one penny of the money to which I had no legal claim ? When you disclosed to me your treachery, you closed to me your purse.

RALPH. But this is madness. You have no right to refuse this money.

STEL. I have a right to refuse from you everything that does not come in the shape of justice. I will not take from your hand as bounty that which it is my privilege to demand of you as a right. I am not ashamed to plead with you to rectify my wrong, but I am ashamed to share it.

RALPH. Why, the most ordinary person would allow——

STEL. I am no ordinary woman, sir; my presence here attests that fact. The world would regard this as unprecedented, and scorn my boldness; but what can I do? a poor and friendless woman; where can I turn for redress ? To the law ? Poverty against wealth weighs but lightly in the scales. And if I won, could damages, wrung from a smiling jury, repay me for the shame speaking in my tears ?

RALPH. If you come for vengeance I have nothing to say. (*turns, sits at table,* R.)

STEL. I did not come for vengeance—I came for justice. I hoped to confess all to the woman you were to wed, and gain her aid ; but the first tone of her voice sealed my lips. I felt she had no heart—she would despise, not pity.

RALPH. Don't speak of her—if you knew my excuse.

STEL. Excuse ! Can you speak to me of an excuse for your act ? Can any pressure of circumstances on your life atone for the ruin of mine ? I am ruined, and can yet face you without a blush, for the shame that has come to me was through your deception, and not my will. You repaid my love with the kiss of a Judas; the ring I wore upon my finger was a mockery—the certificate I guarded as the holy guarantee of my honor was a forgery, and now I have thrown them both away to ask you to replace that spurious metal with the genuine gold.

RALPH. And it was for this you came here ?

STEL. Yes. I would not appeal to your father—I sought not to expose you—and I declined to ask the law for redress.

RALPH. Why ?

STEL. (*sadly*). Because an appeal to the law would but have left as an heirloom to our child a printed record of his father's sin.

RALPH. There—don't speak of him. (*rises, crosses,* L., *sadly.*)

STEL. (*greatly moved*). It is for his sake alone, Ralph, that I am here. Had I to suffer alone I would suffer in silence. I am not pleading to you as a woman for her love, but as a mother for her child. (RALPH *sinks on sofa*) Have you ever thought of him, Ralph—our—your boy? I left him prattling in childish glee, a sunbeam in every smile, a paradise in every toy. We have given him existence, should we not also give him a name? He will one day become a man. Will you force his mother to cloud his future by breathing into his ear, upon the threshold of manhood, the story of a sin? He will one day ask after his father; to say you are dead would be a lie, to whisper you are living would be a shame.

RALPH. Oh, stop—stop.

STEL. Oh, Ralph, do not turn from me—if you no longer love, at least pity me. Remember I am a mother—with all a mother's tenderness, all a mother's love. Oh, think of our boy—I cannot look in his face, I cannot take him in my arms without the thought that he may live to one day curse us both. (*drops on her knees beside him*) Oh, Ralph, be just—give me the right to look in that child's face without a blush—give him the right to call you father.

RALPH. Oh, stop! this is torture. I cannot make redress.

STEL. Cannot! What prevents?

RALPH. Poverty—the loss of my inheritance. Our union would leave me a beggar. (*rises, crosses* R.)

STEL. (*rises*). No man need be a beggar here who has the strength and will to work. You should not shrink from the consequences of your act even though it *be* poverty. I am willing to labor for my child, why should you not labor for the mother?

RALPH. Oh, you do not know. (*sinks in chair,* R.)

CORA *appears,* C., *from park, with letter in her hand. Music, plaintive, pp., till curtain.*

STEL. I know that you have not the courage to do right. But, there, I will plead with you no more. I will leave here forever, and return to my boy. By your act he is orphaned. I will live for his sake and work for his support. I will not make poverty the bugbear of his youth, that he may not plead it as an excuse in his manhood. I will strive to inculcate in his breast a love of truth and a regard for honor, and when, with boyish glee, he speaks as other children of his father, I will bend his knee beside his little cot and point him to his only father—his Father in heaven.

RALPH (R., *springs up, excitedly*). Stella, stop—don't go—I—(CORA *comes down quickly,* C., *he sees her, stops suddenly, sinks on chair, his head on table.*)

CORA (C.). Your dismissal from Mr. Randall, madam. (*gives letter.*)

STEL. (L., *calmly, taking letter*). It comes in good time. Now I am ready to go. (STELLA *stands at door,* L., CORA *stands by ottoman,* C., *looking at her triumphantly,* RALPH *sits* R., *with his head bowed on table. Picture.*)

MEDIUM CURTAIN.

ACT IV.

SCENE.—*Same as Act III.*

Discovery—SEDLEY *sits in chair, at fire, holding a skein of Berlin wool,* EOLA *sits on sofa, winding it off. Lively music at rise.*

EOLA. Are you tired?

SED. Oh, dear, no—not at all. I rather like it.

EOLA. That's funny. My brother Gus. used to get so cross—he never held it half as nice as you do.

SED. Well, brothers don't understand this thing. I never hold it for my sister.

EOLA. You don't! Why?

SED. She don't wind as nice as you do.

EOLA. Oh, Mr. Sedley! (*drops the ball, both stoop for it, their heads come in contact, she draws back timidly*) Oh, excuse me!

SED. (*gives her the ball*). Beg pardon—all my fault. Did I hurt you?

EOLA. Oh, no. How stupid of me to drop the ball!

SED. I was too far off—ought to sit nearer. Don't you think so?

EOLA (*timidly*). I don't know.

SED. (*at end of sofa*) Hadn't I better sit here?

EOLA (*moves to R. end*). Maybe so.

SED. (*sits on other end*). I think that's better; don't you?

EOLA. Yes; it don't wind so tight now.

SED. I wish you wouldn't wind so fast.

EOLA. Yes?

SED. Yes.

EOLA. Why?

SED. You'll get done too soon.

EOLA (*quickly*). Oh, I have a great deal more.

SED. (*sits nearer*). That's jolly! I could sit a whole day and do this.

EOLA. You could?

SED. Yes. (*gets nearer, she looks up, he draws back*). You wind better when I'm close to you, don't you?

EOLA. Ye-s.

SED. Now isn't it funny? Do you know what I was thinking?

EOLA. No.

SED. I was thinking how angry your father would be if he could see us now.

EOLA. Oh, papa's getting old; you mustn't mind him.

SED. No. I won't. (*gets nearer*) He don't like me, does he?

EOLA (*timidly*). He don't know you very well.

SED. Well, you—you knew me very well.

EOLA. Yes.

SED. Well, you like me a little, don't you?

EOLA. Well—I—that is, you have been very kind to me, and I—I always like kind people.

SED. But I don't mean that kind of like; I mean another word like like—same number of letters, but spelt another way.

EOLA. I don't know what you mean?

SED. I mean a word like l-o-v-e. What's that spell?

EOLA. It spells love.

SED. That's it—that's the way I want you to like me. Will you?

EOLA. Oh, my! papa would be so angry.

SED. Oh, your father's getting old; don't mind him.

EOLA. Oh, ain't you ashamed to say that?

SED. I mean, he's older than we are.

EOLA. Of course he is. Oh, Mr. Sedley, you're tangling that all up.

SED. And you're tangling me all up. Come now, say you love me a little, won't you?

EOLA. Not if you say anything against my papa.

SED. Then you do—you do love me a little? (*tries to put arm around her, but can't for the skein.* *Aside*) Confound the skein!

EOLA (*rises*). Oh, dear! you'll have that all in a knot!

SED. (*rises*). Don't go—say yes, won't you?

EOLA Oh, my! some one's coming. Hush! (*she sists* L. *of table,* R., *demurely winding.* SEDLEY *sits on sofa,* L.)

WIMBERLY *enters,* D. R., *with newspaper in his hand, comes* C., *looks at them.*

WIMBERLY. Bless me! what an innocent looking couple! Don't you think you could wind better if you'd sit farther apart?

SED. (*rises*). Good-day, sir; I'm in your way. (*crosses* C.)

WIM. Thank you. I want my favorite chair. Rather chilly in the house. Have you read the morning paper? (*turns arm-chair, sits in front of fire, with his back to them.*)

SED. (R. C.). No, sir. (*aside to* EOLA) He's in a good humor; isn't he! EOLA. Yes; splendid!

WIM. (*reads paper*). Never ought to miss reading a morning paper, sir—greatest blessing of an enlightened age.

SED. Yes, sir; you're right, sir. (*to her*) May I ask him?

EOLA. If you want to.

WIM. Paper full of news. A conductor on the Third Avenue line was robbed of all the fares last night. The directors call it sacrilege, and intend having detectives hereafter on each car.

SED. That's too bad.

WIM. Bad! Egad, I think that robbery was a blessing.

SED. Of course, sir; that's what I mean.

EOLA. Don't contradict him.

SED. (*places skein in her lap, with sudden resolve*). Here—hold this. I'll ask him right away. (*goes* L., *boldly.*)

WIM. Bless me; listen to this. (*reads,* SEDLEY *stops,* C.) "The bill now before the legislature at Albany, by which it is proposed to increase the head money paid to the Commissioners of Emigration for every emigrant landed at Castle Garden, is calculated to inflict serious injury upon the commerce of this port, as the steamship companies are unanimous in their determination to land their passengers at Boston and other ports, rather than submit to the additional tax."

SED. (*retreating to* EOLA). He won't listen to me.

WIM. Well, sir, what do you think of that?

SED. It's terrible, sir. The emigrants ought to know better.

WIM. (*springs up*). Emigrants the devil, sir. What have they to do with it? It's your greedy politicians, filling their pockets, and driving a prosperous trade from your city; can't you see that?

EOLA (*aside*). Oh, dear, don't ask him now.

SED. I—I was thinking of something else.

WIM Why, confound it, then you didn't hear a word.

SED. Oh, yes, sir. I heard it; but the fact is——

WIM. You didn't understand it.

EOLA. Of course, papa, he understood it, but I took away his attention. My Berlin wool got all tangled up.

SED. (*desperate*). The fact is, Mr. Wimberly, I wish—hem! I wish to speak to you on a very serious subject.

WIM. Well, sir, go on.

SED. I have seen, that is, I have felt—of course you are well aware—well, when I say I feel, I mean to say——

WIM. That you have a sensation, eh?

SED. Yes, sir; a sensation in a way—a feeling in a way—that I feel bound—of course to tell you—but that you might——

WIM. Why, bless me, Mr Sedley, you're tangled up worse than the wool.

SED. Can't get started, sir. Would you mind a little walk? I think I can talk better in the air.

WIM. Bless me, I hope so. Come at once, sir, if you please. (*goes up, C.*)

SED. (*to* EOLA). He's in a bad humor now, isn't he?

EOLA (*rises*). No, only pretending.

WIM. (*at window*). I'm waiting, sir.

ELLA *enters*, D. R., *with package of blank letters tied nicely with white ribbon.*

SED. (*going up*). Good day, Miss Ella; I'm just going to take a little stroll with Mr. Wimberly.

ELLA. Well, go on; I have no objections.

                  [WIMBERLY *and* SEDLEY *go out*, C.

EOLA. Oh, Ella, I am so happy.

ELLA. Are you? I'm glad somebody's happy here. (*goes* R, *sits at desk.*)

EOLA. Are you going to write?

ELLA. No, only send away some antiquities. (*directs the package.*)

EOLA. Antiquities?

ELLA. Yes—musty old love letters.

EOLA (*goes to her*). Oh, my, you're not going to give up your love letters?

ELLA. Of course I am; what's the good of them when the subject's worn out?

EOLA. Oh, dear, I'd never do that.

ELLA. Pshaw! Every girl has to do it some time. I—I expected how it would be from the first—I—I thought it would end like this; so I bought this—this pretty piece of ribbon, and kept them tied up nice so as to have them all ready when the time came to send them back.

EOLA. I wouldn't do it, dear.

ELLA (*rises, goes to table*). Oh, you're a child—you don't understand these things. (*rings bell on table.*)

EOLA. Well, I'm commencing to learn.

Enter SERVANT, D. L.

ELLA. Leave this package at Mrs. Malvernon's. There is no answer.

             [SERVANT *takes letter, and exits*, D. L.

There, now, it's done, and I—I am wretched. (*sinks on ottoman, C.*)

EOLA (*goes to her*). I'm so sorry you're unhappy.

ELLA. I'm not unhappy. Do you think I—I care because I sent back some—some old letters.

EOLA. It seems so strange. I'm sure I'd never send back a love letter.

ELLA. Did you ever have one?

EOLA. No—not yet.

ELLA. You think they are wonderful—but they're not. I'll show you one.

EOLA. Why, didn't you send them all away ?

ELLA (*takes letter from dress*). No—I—I retained just one—to remember how—how badly he wrote. Listen to this. (*reads*) " My dear Jap " —He used to call me Jap because my hair came out—" My dear Jap— I am thinking of you, and hard at work. I'm painting the handsomest monkey you ever saw. I can't take you out boating to-day ; the monkey's leg is most done, and I hate to leave off Excuse and think of me in solitude. Be very careful of your hair ; a bald young lady is not interesting, and a wig is not artistic. Thine in Cupid.—Fred." There what do you think of that '

EOLA. I think it's horrid !

ELLA (*rises*) Well, if you don't like his letters, Miss Wimberly, you might keep it to yourself. (*crosses*, R., *angrily.*)

EOLA. I mean I don't think Albery would write like that.

ELLA. Are you speaking of Mr. Sedley ?

EOLA (*timidly*). Yes. He's gone to ask papa to let me call him Albery.

ELLA. Well, upon my word you are going fast.

EOLA. You told me to commence early.

ELLA. Did I ? Well, I've changed my mind. (*sits*, R. H.) I thought I knew the men, and I didn't.

EOLA. All men are not alike.

ELLA. Oh bother. Every girl thinks her lover is perfect. You take my advice—let the men alone. I've had more experience than you have, and if I can't manage them—you can't.

Enter RALPH, D. R.

EOLA. I don't want to manage them. (*sees* RALPH) Oh !

RALPH. Don't let me disturb you. Talking secrets ? (*crosses to fire.*)

EOLA. Oh no—I was just going—I want to see—papa. (*to* ELLA) Don't tell, Ella. (*aside, going up*) Everybody has the blues in this house but me—and I—oh I am *so* happy. [*Exit*, c., *on lawn.*

ELLA. Is anything the matter, Ralph ?

RALPH. Yes. I'm going away.

ELLA. Going away ? (*rises, goes to him.*)

RALPH. Yes. My father gives me a home simply upon a condition ; I have been base enough to hesitate, but I have at last summoned the courage to go.

ELLA. Is it about Cora ?

RALPH. Yes. I have resolved not to make her my wife.

ELLA. Oh I'm so glad, Ralph ; I don't like her.

RALPH. I sought this opportunity, Ella, to speak of some one else ; a young man who I find has suffered through me.

ELLA. Who do you mean ?

RALPH. Fred Town.

ELLA. Excuse me, I don't want to hear anything about that person. (*goes*, c., *sits on ottoman.*

RALPH (*goes to her*). I am altogether to blame for what has happened, and you must listen to me. There has been a mistake, and before I go I wish to show you Fred in his true light.

ELLA. If you want to eulogize Mr. Town, go to the lady who will take most pleasure in hearing it.

RALPH. And who is that ?

ELLA. Mrs. Lee.

RALPH. That lady has already a correct conception of his character, and values him highly.

ELLA. I've no doubt of it.

RALPH. I am not only aware of her friendship, but also approve of it.

ELLA. Oh! Then you are interested in this fair widow too?

RALPH (*calmly*). I have a right to be, since I propose making her my wife.

ELLA (*springs up*). What!

RALPH. I am prepared for your surprise, but let me tell you frankly, I am not prepared for any explanation. I have but one object in telling you this, Ella, to show you that you have wronged Mr. Town.

ELLA. I don't wish you to apologize for Mr. Town. The fact that you are his successful rival don't compel you to get him a wife. (*crosses to fire.*)

RALPH. There was no question of rivalry between us, and as this may be our last interview, I must request you to respect my words. Fred Town is as true and noble a gentleman as lives, and far more honorable —than your brother.

ELLA (*comes to him, takes his hand*). Ralph!

RALPH. It is true. Here, sit there. Turn your face away from me. (*seats her on sofa, stands R. of her*) A man who has to confess a guilty secret should not look in the eyes of a pure woman. I had hoped to convince you without wholly exposing myself, but I will not suffer a noble man to be compromised by my act. This Mrs. Lee is not a widow. She is a noble girl with a secret in her life, and with which secret *I am unworthily connected*. As I sank in the mire Fred Town came to that poor girl's rescue, and placed her feet upon firm ground. He stood by her as a friend, preserved her secret at the risk of his own happiness, and placed her in a position to reach my heart. This is the sole interest Mr. Town has had in Mrs Lee; an interest actuated through sympathy and continued through honor.

ELLA (*sadly*). And I not know.

Music, plaintive, pp. RANDALL *appears,* C.

RALPH. His loyalty to her secret made him appear disloyal to you. The sole cause of all this trouble stands before you—your unworthy brother. Don't look at me—I could not bear to go away with the sight of the scorn flashing in those eyes. Let me leave without a kiss, without even a pressure of the hand. I wish to carry with me, in my exile, the remembrance of your face as I saw it before you had learned to blush for me. Good-bye, Ella, my dear sister; I dare not hope for sympathy—I cannot expect pardon. All I can ask is, that you will try and forget that the shadow of your brother's sin once raised a passing cloud between you and your love. (*going,* R.)

ELLA. Ralph, don't go; I forgive you *all*. (*she rushes to him, he folds her in his arms, kisses her brow.* RANDALL *comes down,* L. C.)

RANDALL (*sternly*). Ella, come here! (*she goes to him, slowly*) I have no longer a son; for the future you will forget that you ever had a brother.

ELLA. Oh, papa! no—you don't——

RAN. I wish no comments upon my conduct, please. Leave us. (*goes down to fire,* ELLA *goes slowly to door,* L., *turns, looking at* RALPH.)

ELLA. Ralph, all my soul speaks to you in my last words. Good-bye.

[*Exit,* D. L. *Music stops.*

Ran. (*standing at fire*). I see you have had the good taste to take your sister into your confidence.

Ralph (R.). I was compelled to do so.

Ran. The sympathies of a young girl are easily excited, and as a man of the world I presume you know every note in the scale.

Ralph. A man who is utterly defensive, sir, is unworthy your sarcasm.

Ran. You are right—accept my apology. From what I heard as I entered, I presume you are about to leave here.

Ralph. Do you wish me to remain?

Ran. That is bad taste, sir—I hate to have a man answer a question by asking another.

Ralph. Well, sir, I leave here at once, since you drive me from the house.

Ran. I deny that; you drive yourself out.

Ralph. Very well, father; in either case I am ready to go, and at once.

Ran. One moment, please.

Ralph. There is nothing further to be said, is there?

Ran. Yes, sir, there is something further to be said. This—woman has dared to enter my house, and appears to set my authority at defiance; her influence over you is apparent from this letter, in which you grandly take leave of me, and regret your inability to follow my wishes. (*produces letter.*)

Ralph. I wrote you that because I thought further words between us could do no good.

Ran. Did I consider only my outraged feelings, I would never trouble myself to speak to you again; but I have determined—I confess after a struggle—to have more consideration for you than you have ever had for me.

Ralph (*quickly*). Oh, father—will you forgive?

Ran. Never, sir, while I have memory and will. You have forced me to break my word—you turn your back upon Miss Adair, the daughter of my old friend, and a woman worthy, in every respect, to be your wife. You have destroyed the greatest wish of my life, and now propose to leave here with the woman who has brought her shame across my door.

Ralph. Any shame there may be in the matter, father, rests solely upon me. Knowledge and intention are necessary to every sin. This poor girl believed herself my wife; is her soul less pure that she believed a lie?

Ran. I decline to discuss this question with you, sir. Some time since you charged me, I believe, with not having faithfully performed my duty as a father.

Ralph. For all that I may have said in a hasty moment, sir, I beg your pardon.

Ran. You assert that your collegiate education will not supply you with the experience necessary to earn your bread; but you will please remember that I educated you for the position of a man of wealth not called upon to earn your living. A loving father, proud of his son, is not likely to anticipate that boy's villainy, and make provision for his graduating in crime. My respect for my word compels me to cast you out of my heart forever, but I will not leave you altogether a beggar. (*crosses, R., sits at desk.*)

Ralph (C). What do you mean?

Ran. (*writes in check-book*). I mean that I will atone for my fault in educating you so well, by placing you in possession of a sum large enough to enable you to live until you can learn sufficient to earn your bread. Here is a check upon my bankers for $2,000. Take it. (*tears check from book, rises—extends it to him.*)

RALPH. I thank you. sir—but I prefer not.

RAN. What! you refuse ?

RALPH. Yes, father, I refuse. In having the courage to do what is right, I am prepared to face the consequences. I am willing to work, but, while I have health and strength, I will not beg.

RAN. I'm not asking you to beg, sir. I *give* you this. Remember, it is all you will ever get from me. At my death this estate will be divided between my daughter and Miss Adair. Then take this. (*with some emotion*) Come, Ralph—*I wish you to have it.*

RALPH. It is useless, sir; I will not accept one penny of your money unaccompanied with your blessing. The fear of being deprived of my inheritance has made me what I am ; the resolve to act without any thought of it has made me a free man. Farewell, father—I am sorry I have not been to you a more worthy son. Do not quite curse me. Remember that, by becoming the husband of Miss Adair, I would forever close the door of atonement to the woman I have wronged. Good-bye, father ; I will not forget you, though I start now upon a road that will separate us forever.

Goes slowly to door, R. FRED *enters*, C.

RAN. You absolutely refuse to take this then ?

RALPH. Absolutely, sir.   [*Exit*, D. L.

FRED (*comes down*, C.). Is Ralph going away ?

RAN. (*sharply*). Yes, sir—he's going away—have you any objections ? (*going to door*, R.)

FRED. I have no right to object.

RAN. In that case, sir, I must ask you not to trouble me with any questions.   [*Exit*, D. R.

FRED. There goes a modern edition of the paternal Brutus. I don't think playing the part of Sir Pandarus suits me. I have come to the conclusion that meddling in other people's business is not just the proper way of advancing your own. That old gentleman will never forgive my connection with this matter. Confound it, he's hard as steel. Achilles was vulnerable in the heel, but this man appears all armor.

ELLA *enters*, D. L., FRED *sees her, goes to table, sits* R. *of it, takes up book.*

Hem ! Now for it.

ELLA (*comes down* C., *timidly*). Mr. Town.

FRED. Did you speak to me ?

ELLA. Yes.

FRED. I thought I heard you mention my name—I wasn't quite sure though—used to call me Fred, you know.

ELLA. That would be difficult now.

FRED. Well, I suppose you're out of practice.

ELLA. I—I might get in practice again.

FRED. That's true—so you might.

ELLA. Is your book interesting ?

FRED. Very.

ELLA. If you did not hold it upside down you might find it more so.

FRED. Hem ! Well, no—this story is dull—I always read a dull story upside down.

ELLA. Indeed.

FRED. Yes. You see the difficulty of interpreting one word makes it interesting to find the meaning of the next.

ELLA. I presume then, that's the way you read my letters.

FRED. Well, no—I had trouble enough to read them anyway.

ELLA. Indeed!

FRED. You see, you had that horid habit of crossing and re-crossing the paper, making it difficult to tell where one sentence began and the other ended.

ELLA. They must have been terribly dull.

FRED. On the contrary—But alas, they have gone from me, like a summer dream.

ELLA. Would you like to read them again? (*takes a package of letters from her pocket; they are different from the first package, and are tied with a common string.*)

FRED. Be delighted.

ELLA. There. (*places package timidly on his lap.*)

FRED. (*aside*). Propitious powers—Juno relents.

ELLA. I want to exchange them.

FRED. What for?

ELLA (*shyly*). For yours.

FRED. You sent mine back; I can't return them.

ELLA. Why not?

FRED. I never keep rejected "MSS," so I burnt them.

ELLA. Oh, Fred! (*goes L., in tears.*)

FRED (*rises*). Yes, I burnt them. The flames crackled amid the rose-colored paper; the forked tongues darted out at me, mocking my hopes; the black symbols that spoke my love vanished in the air, and naught remained but the product of combustion, carbonic acid, and ashes. The chemical element I could not keep—it had gone to whisper my folly to the flowers; but the ashes remained—I reverently collected them with a silver spoon and placed them——

ELLA. Where?

FRED. In a snuff-box. (*takes out handsome snuff-box.*)

ELLA. You're laughing at me.

FRED. The snuff-box is a new one; I would not permit the odor of the nicotine leaf to cling around the embalmed remembrance of my love.

ELLA. If the letters are gone, what good are the ashes.

FRED. As a souvenir. They serve to remind me that I once gave a woman the power to throw back in my teeth the vows of love penned by an honest hand.

ELLA. Give me my letters.

FRED. No, I'll keep them. (*puts them in his pocket.*)

ELLA. Where; in a snuff-box?

FRED. Precisely. In their place I give you this. In this little casket rest the letters I once wrote to you, but in a changed form. Upon the lid I have inscribed the following beautiful elegy:—(*reads from snuff-box.*)

> Pandora gave to man a box,
> From out it young hope dashes;
> It leads a man until he finds
> His love and hope are—ashes.

ELLA. You're making fun of me, and it's cruel; but it's always the way with you men; if a woman frowns, you are kneeling at her feet, but if she smiles, you are striking at her heart. (*sits on sofa, sobs.*)

FRED. And when she weeps, we are nestling by her side. You asked me for my letters—take them. There, don't turn away; I am in earnest. This little box is not elegant, but it is truthful, and it contains a lesson we may both profit by. Take it, Ella, and with it the assurance that my love, Phœnix-like, but springs rejuvenated from its—ashes. (*kneels beside her.*)

ELLA (*takes box*). Fred, I've—I've been very naughty.

FRED. Good!

ELLA. And I'm—I'm sorry now.

FRED. Better!

ELLA. And I'll never do so any more.

FRED. Best.

ELLA. You forgive me?

FRED. Fully.

ELLA. Oh, Fred! (*falls in his arms.*)

FRED. Oh, Ella!

WIMBERLY *and* EOLA *enter*, C. EOLA *goes down* R., *sulkily.* FRED *and* ELLA *spring up.*

WIMBERLY (C.). Bless me—what's all this?

FRED (L. C.). Rehearsal, sir; we're practicing for private theatricals. (ELLA *crosses* R, *to* EOLA.)

WIM. Well, sir, if you *act* as naturally as you rehearse, your performance will be a success. Come here, I want to talk to you. (*they stand by fire*)

ELLA. Oh, dear, I'm so happy!

EOLA (*turns, sits sulkily at table*). Are you? Well, I'm glad some one's happy here.

ELLA. Why, what's the matter?

EOLA. Why, I'm—I'm wretched.

ELLA. My poor darling! Your father has refused Mr. Sedley.

EOLA. No, he hasn't.

ELLA. No? Then what is it?

EOLA. Why, he's—he's put it off ever so long.

ELLA. What, the marriage?

EOLA. Yes. Papa told Albery that if he'd come to Chicago, set up in business, and ask for me again at the end of five years, then—he'd *think of it!*

ELLA. And what did Mr. Sedley say?

EOLA. Said he didn't think his father would let him.

ELLA. Well, don't fret; it will all come right.

EOLA. No, it won't. You can't expect a man to be true five years.

ELLA. Oh, yes, you can. When a man truly loves, he's one of nature's noblemen, and you can safely trust him.

EOLA (*looks up, surprised*). Gracious! you've changed your views wonderfully.

ELLA. Yes. I've been taking lessons in manology, and it's done me good. But come, let's go out in the park; I ve lots to tell you.

They go up, meeting RANDALL, *who enters*, D. R., *he bows coldly, goes down, sits at desk, writing.*

EOLA. What's the matter with your father?

ELLA. He's got the blues.

EOLA. How I pity him! [EOLA *and* ELLA *go off*, C.

WIM. (*to* FRED). Now's our time. You go look to your part of the work, I'll vouch for mine. .

FRED. I'll have all ready in five minutes. [*Exit* FRED, D. L.

WIM. (*back to fire*). Busy, Walter?

RANDALL (*writing*). Not very. Why?

WIM. I want to talk to you.

RAN. Talk away; I can write and listen. Nothing very serious, I hope.

WIM. Yes, it is serious. You've sent Ralph away.

RAN. I thought it was *your* business you wished to speak of.

WIM. (*goes* c.). Come, now, Walter, that's unkind. You and I have been old friends for years, and you know that I am interested in all that concerns your happiness.

RAN. (*places letter in envelope, directs it*). I have abandoned all hope of happiness.

WIM. Yes, that's it; just like most men. Drive happiness away through your stubbornness, and then complain over being wretched. Now, you are unhappy because you have abandoned your son.

RAN. Excuse me, William, but this is a matter that concerns me alone. (*rises, crosses,* L.)

WIM. (R. C.). There, you can't stop me by any display of dignity. I'm not only your friend, but I'm your son's friend, and I'm not going to stand by and see him shoved out of this house without saying, at least, that it's a damned shame.

RAN. I consider myself the best judge in this matter, and, I believe, understand my duty. (*sits on sofa.*)

WIM. Duty! duty be—— There, you shan't spoil my case by making me angry. What do you call duty—sending your son away because he can't mould his heart according to your fancy?

RAN. Before you appear in his defence you should know all the points in the case.

WIM. I do know them, Walter; I know that Ralph has acted wrong—confoundedly wrong; but he has a plenty of good, solid stuff at bottom, and I don't want to see it turned to clay.

RAN. If you know all, can you blame me?

WIM. Certainly, I can. You may change iron into any shape you will, but you must heat it before you commence beating it with a hammer. You should take your boy by the hand, warm his heart by the electric spark of paternal sympathy, and try to lead him, not drive.

RAN. I have no belief in the system of coaxing. A son's first duty is obedience.

WIM. Very true, Walter; but remember youth is rather hasty and prompt to go wrong. A father may regret a son's yielding to temptation, but he should not drive that son to, perhaps, worse deeds, by any uncalled for severity.

RAN. I have explained to him my wishes, and he has seen fit to despise them.

WIM. You're begging the question, Walter. You permit your selfishness and pride to blind you.

RAN. (*springs up*). Sir!

WIM. There—don't jump—in severe cases the doctor must use the knife. Let us look this thing full in the face. In your selfish desire to have your wishes carried out, you forget the suffering that may be entailed upon another. Now, what is your son doing? He is striving to make the only atonement in his power for a vile wrong to an innocent girl, and has thrown away his inheritance in order to act like an honorable man.

RAN. Look here—answer me plainly—what is it you would have me do?

WIM. Reconcile yourself to the inevitable, pardon your son, and receive him here with his wife.

RAN. You forget yourself, sir—that woman—— (*crosses, sits at table.*)

Music—STELLA *appears at window, comes slowly down,* C.

WIM. That, lady, sir, whose purity and suffering entitles her at least to respect. (*takes her hand*) She has been an innocent party in all of this. She has come here to seek your son, but before leaving she wishes to ask your forgiveness. (*nods to* STELLA, *who goes* R. C., *kneels at side of* RANDALL.)

STEL. To beg it, sir, on my knees.

RAN. (*rises*). You here?

WIM. I requested Mr. Town to send this lady here, feeling that as a gentleman, you would at least listen to her.

RAN. My letter to you, madam, I believe conveyed my wishes.

STEL. (*rises*). I could not resist the opportunity, sir, of seeing you, if only for once, in my true character, and asking your pardon for my deception.

RAN. I must ask you to spare me any supplications.

STEL. I do not intend to supplicate, sir—I wish simply to make you a confession of the whole truth, and show you that I am at least worthy of your sympathy.

RAN. I can really see no good in all this. (*sits against* L. *of table.*)

STEL. Do not refuse me at least the satisfaction of knowing that you have heard the whole truth? I have entered your house under a false name, and for that deception I ask your pardon. In the desire to right myself, I have wronged you. (WIMBERLY *stands* L., *at fire, listening.*)

RAN. I am sorry you wish to dwell upon the subject.

STEL. Do not think harshly of me; I am only weakly striving to justify myself in your eyes. My father was a Virginian, residing on a little property near Nomini Court House, Westmoreland County. There I was born. My mother died when I was very young, and my father, impoverished by the war, removed to Richmond, where he obtained some little employment as a civil engineer. Some years after, receiving a lucrative offer to go to England, he left this country, taking me with him.

RAN. All this is useless——

STEL. Oh, do not refuse to listen to me, sir—the only defence I can make, is to tell you the plain story of my life.

RAN. (*slightly moved*). Well—go on.

STEL. We reached London in safety, and after a few days rest started for our final destination, Manchester. The train started, and father and I were alone in the carriage in which the guard had locked us. It was a stormy night, the rain poured in torrents; but the train dashed on, with what seemed to me, like reckless speed. My father fell asleep, and I was left alone with my thoughts. The darkness without was impenetrable, that within was only relieved by the feeble light of a small lamp. The only sound was the monotonous rumble of the wheels over their iron bed. The solitude became painful—I was afraid—my mind began to wander—I thought I heard strange whispers; faces appeared laughing at me through the windows—I leaned over to arouse my father from his sleep, when there was a violent rocking of the carriage, a sudden jerk—a shriek from the engine, a cry of human agony—and then—all was darkness.

RAN. (*interested*). An accident.

STEL. When I recovered my senses, I was lying upon the side of the road, a man was standing near me, holding a lantern in his hand; but at my side, kneeling upon the wet ground, was a younger man, who held my wounded head tenderly upon his knee. I looked up wondering in his face, and I saw for the first time, sir—your son.

Ran. Well.

Stel. All was again a blank, and when after days of delirium, I crawled back to strength, I learned that I was alone in a strange land, for in the darkness that came upon me that fatal night, I had lost my all, my father.

Ran. (*moved*). Go on.

Stel. The only face that was not strange to me, was the face of your son. He had remained to guard me, had paid for the lodging in which I slept, and when he learned my utter helplessness, gradually breathed into my ear the interest he felt in my fate, and—offered me his hand.

Ran. (*sadly*). Which you accepted.

Stel. What was I to do? I was alone, without money, without friends. He had seen to the interment of my poor father's body, my father torn from me in my sleep, and buried without a daughter's presence or a daughter's kiss. It was your son who found him a grave, and paid him the last testimony of respect. It was your son who stood by me in my helplessness, tended me with the gentle care of a woman, and when in return for his devotions he asked me for my love—oh, sir, can you wonder that I said, yes?

Ran. Go on—go on.

Stel. I knew him but as Ralph Gordon. He spoke of his father as a man of pride and wealth, and urged upon me a secret marriage, to be only acknowledged when he had prevailed upon his father to accept his bride. I loved him and accepted, and we were married at night in a little chapel near my father's grave.

Ran. And then?

Stel. We returned to this country, where in a little home in Eatentown, I found perfect happiness, until that night when he fled, leaving behind him the penned confession of his sin. His letter would have killed me, but the thought of my child made me strong. In my utter need, Heaven sent me one friend, who listened to my plea, and brought me here. There, sir, is the worthless certificate I received at my father's grave. I came here to ask your son for justice; I have told you all, and though I have taken from you your boy—oh, sir—have I not a right to him? (*sinks on her knees.*)

Ran. (*rises, raises her*). Rise, madam. I confess I have done you gross injustice in my thoughts, and I am sorry for it. I find my son was not led into error, but has been a deliberate villain.

Stel. He wished me to tell you all. He is sorry—he is seeking to atone.

Ran. His only atonement will be in making you his wife; but in doing that he separates himself from me forever.

Wim. Why, confound it, Walter, you don't mean——

Ran. I must request you not to interrupt me, sir. I am not so utterly heartless as you imagine. I have here a letter (*shows the one he wrote at desk*) to my bankers, placing the sum of $5,000 to his credit; if he does not use it, it will go to his child. I will have no hard thoughts for you, madam, but my son has deceived me, and I will not break my word—at my death my estate will be equally divided between my daughter, Ella, and the daughter of my old friend, Adair.

Stel. (*calmly*). You cannot leave anything to his child.

Ran. What do you mean?

Stel. I mean that the child of Mr. Adair is—dead.

Ran. (*starts*). What! (Wimberly *stands, quietly,* L.)

Stel. I speak the truth, sir; the lady who is here bears his name, but is not his child.

Ran. Pray, madam, do you expect me to believe this? (*rings bell on table.*)

Wim. (*quickly*). What are you going to do?

Ran. Summon Miss Adair to answer this charge.

Stel. That will be her triumph, sir, for I have no proof.

Ran. Then why do you dare to accuse her?

Stel. To save you from the deception that she has practiced upon you for years. I had proof in Mr. Buddles; he has disappeared. Now, sir, grant me one favor—the only one—the last. Leave me alone with that woman, but overhear our conversation—if she does not betray herself, do with me as you will.

Ran. You wish to make me a spy?

Wim. If she is really Miss Adair there can be no injury to her; if she is not, she ought to be found out.

Stel. I know she is deceiving you, sir. I can only hope to unmask her in this way—grant me the trial.

Ran. (*slight pause*). I consent.

Servant *enters*, D. R.

Robert, tell Miss Adair I wish to see her.

Wim. Hem! No—say *a* lady, but not what lady.

Ran. Very well—do so.   [Servant *exits*, D. R.

Come, sir, let us go. I am consenting to an arrangement, madam, that I am ashamed of, but I must know how much truth there is in all this. (*goes up and off*, C.)

Wim. (*as he goes up, to* Stella). Keep up your courage; for Heaven's sake, don't fail.   [*Exit*, C.

Stel. Now that what I wished for is in my grasp, I tremble so I can hardly stand. Oh, if I but knew how to choose my words. If I can only save that poor old man from this adventuress, I will at least have done some good. If Mr. Town had but obtained some proof—if but one line——

Cora *enters*, D. R.—*starts*. Stella *stands* L. C.

Cora. Robert told me a lady was waiting   he must have been mistaken.

Stel. (*calmly*). It is I who wished to see you, Miss Adair.

Cora. You will permit me to confess my surprise at seeing you here?

Stel. I am here because I have something to say to you alone.

Cora. You can have nothing to say to me that others should not hear.

Stel. I will tell you.

Cora. Thank you—I don't take servants into my confidence.

Stel. (*calmly*). Are you sure of that?

Cora. I believe I understand my own character.

Stel. I am glad of that—my task will be less difficult.

Cora. Your pardon. We have nothing in common, and I refuse to listen to your communication. We do not stand upon equal ground; and, until you leave this house, I will seek the protection of my room. If you have anything to say to me, I prefer it should be in writing. (*going.*)

Stel. (*quietly*). And to whom shall I address my letter—Cora Adair, or—Jane Waters?

Cora (*slight start*). I am at a loss to understand you.

Stel. If you will remain I will take pleasure in explaining.

Cora. Thank you, but I can hardly feel enough interest in it to remain longer in your presence.

Stel. You prefer, then, that I should take my information to Mr. Randall?

Cora (*comes down*, R. C.). That implies a threat. Pray don't misunderstand me. I desired to free myself from your presence, not to fly from your information; as you appear to believe that I am intimidated, however, I will remain. (*looks quickly around, and sits L. of table*) Please spare me any prosy oration, and make your accusation as brief as possible.

Stel. I have no accusation to make; I simply wish to tear a leaf from the past, and hand it to you as your passport to another sphere of action.

Cora. My dear madam—I will call you madam,—while being concise pray be intelligible. I have a horror of riddles.

Stel. I will endeavor to be plain; but first let me make a confession. When I first saw you I disliked you. At that time I knew nothing against you, and I had no just cause for my antipathy. It was an unworthy feeling, springing from purely selfish motives; and, as I wronged you then, I now ask your pardon.

Cora. Don't trouble yourself to apologize.

Stel. I do so in justice to my better nature. At the time to which I allude you intimated that you would drive me from this house; I will be less harsh than you, and simply request you to leave.

Cora. Request me to leave? Really I must do you the justice to admire your assurance.

Stel. I ask you to leave this house in order that you may be spared the pain of having its master tell you to go.

Cora (*rises*). Madam, you go too far!

Stel. If you will kindly remain seated I will give you my reasons.

Cora. Well, in doing so, pray spare me your insults. (*sits.*)

Stel. If what I say insults you, you can only blame yourself. I suggested to you the propriety of leaving this house, because you fill a position here to which you have no claim.

Cora. Go on. You may excite my contempt; I will not permit you to arouse my anger.

Stel. As you are evidently determined to test my power, I must trouble you to listen to a short narration of facts. Mr. Randall had, in his youth, a friend to whom he was ardently attached. Failure in business drove that friend into exile, and for many years all trace of him was lost, until one day a letter was brought by a young girl, which proved to be a message from the dead. From that letter Mr. Randall learned that his friend had died in India, with but little means, and consigned to him, as the bearer of the missive, his only child. It breathed, in sad tones, the story of his misfortunes, the death of his wife, the loss of his property, and concluded with the request of a dying man, that his old friend would not forget the pledge in their youth as to the future of their children.

Cora. I am thoroughly acquainted with my history, I believe.

Stel. That is but the surface of the story; I will now go to the depths. Mr. Randall received that child as a sacred trust, gave her a home, surrounded her with luxury, and, in the desire to carry out the promise of his youth, sought to make her the wife of his son.

RANDALL *and* WIMBERLY *appear at window.*

Cora. We are still on the surface; all this is well known.

Stel. True; but it is not so well known that Mr. Randall has been shamefully deceived in all this ; that he has never seen the daughter of his friend

Cora. That is strange, since I am here.

Stel. (*aside*). Oh, will I never break through her coldness ! (*aloud*) It is not strange when the facts are known. The daughter of Adair died a short time after her father, leaving her letter in the hands of one unscrupulous enough to use it.

Cora. If this is true—who am I ?

Stel. Jane Waters ! sheltered by that poor, dead girl, that you might one day betray her father's friend.

Cora (*strives to be calm*). This is really becoming interesting. Pray, proceed.

Stel. (*aside*). Oh, I shall fail—she is ice. (*aloud*) Have I given you sufficient reasons why you should leave here ?

Cora. You have given reasons enough, if they were true—unfortunately they lack one essential element—proof.

Stel. I would scarcely make such a statement if I were unable to prove it.

Cora (*aside*). It's impossible—she can't have it ! (*aloud*) And what is the nature of this proof ?

Stel. The testimony of the dead man's confidential clerk, Mr. Buddles.

Cora (*relieved*). In order to make his testimony available, you must first produce him.

Stel. (*quickly*). You have forced him to fly.

Cora. It does not matter, since he has gone.

Stel. His absence is evidence of my truth.

Cora. And what does it prove ? Let us look at this matter fairly. We are rivals for a gentleman's love ; you assume the part of accuser—you have no proof—it is simply a question of veracity—your word against mine. Now, when you consider our relative positions, which of us, do you think, stands the best chance of being believed ? (Randall comes down, c., *very slowly*.)

Stel. My word would count but little, but a letter——

Cora (*starts*). What letter ?

Stel. (*excitedly*). Your letter to Mr. Buddles—promising a reward for his silence.

Cora (*starts up, violently excited*). It's false ! he burnt——(*stops, confused.*)

Stel. (*turns quickly*). The test is over, sir ; *has it failed ?* (*points to* Cora)

Cora (*starts*). Mr. Randall ! (*pause.* Randall *stands sternly,* c.)

Ran. I am grieved to have been a witness to this scene—more so at its unexpected termination. After what has occurred, it is hardly necessary for me to request you to retire.

Cora. Why, you can't believe all this—let her produce the letter.

Stel. Mr. Buddles told Mr. Town of the letter ; I have never seen it.

Ran. No further proof is necessary. Your manner throughout the controversy has been a tacit avowal of guilt. Your presence hereafter will be painful to me, and I must request you at your earliest convenience, to leave this house. (*sinks on sofa,* L., *agitated.*)

Cora. Very well, sir; I will not supplicate. As you prefer the word of that woman to the assertion of a lady, I trust she will compensate you for my absence. (*aside, at* D. R.) Failure at last—and through *her !*

[*Exit,* D. R.

RALPH, FRED, ELLA, *and* EOLA, *appear at window*, WIMBERLY, *having beckoned to them, goes down*, L. *of sofa*.

WIM. Walter—my old friend—they are here.

RAN. Don't speak—look at me—I am a helpless old man, deceived on all sides—can you ask me after this to trust in human love ! (*music, pp., plaintive.*)

STEL. (*comes slowly to sofa*). We are going now, sir. I have done my duty, yet even in that I have caused you pain. I have exposed a woman whom you loved, and I have robbed you of a son in whom you once had pride. A poor and friendless girl, I have been thrown by fate within the shadow of your life, and my presence has caused nothing but pain. As a mother, struggling for her child, I may have your sympathy—but, as the wife of your son, I dare not ask your blessing. Farewell, sir ; you have forbidden us to love you, but I at least will pray for you (*goes up slowly*, R)

WIM. Walter, crush down this pride—for Heaven's sake call her back !

RANDALL *sits, greatly moved, his head bowed*. RALPH *comes slowly down*.

RALPH. Father ! (RANDALL *slightly starts*) Let me call you so the last time. I am about to leave here—perhaps forever. I am going, hand in hand, with the woman I have wronged. She has told you all I have been guilty of ; you know how much I have to atone. I have been to you in every way unworthy—but try and forgive, if you can't forget. I am not pleading now for the sake of your money—I am no longer afraid of the future ; but, in order that my life may not be altogether clouded by the remembrance of your sternness, say to me but once, as a father to a son—"God bless you—good-bye." (*extends his hand*—RANDALL *rises, shaking with emotion, and, without looking at* RALPH, *takes his hand.*)

RAN. My boy, I cannot say—good-bye—I can only say—bring to me your wife.

STEL. (*rushes down to him with a cry*). Father !

RAN. My child.

STELLA *kneels at* RANDALL'S *feet ; he stands* L. C., *with left hand on her head the right hand extended to* RALPH, *who stands behind her ;* WIMBERLY *stands at fire, rubbing his hands ;* FRED *at window, seizes* ELLA *in his arms ;* EOLA *turns from them with a pout, and sits at piano— plays. Picture.*

CURTAIN.

SYNOPSIS.

THE scene of Act I. is laid in the garden of a small cottage in Eatentown, N. J., known as Gordon Villa. The proprietor is a MR. RALPH GORDON, who occupies it in company with his wife, STELLA, and child. He is apparently a man of leisure, having, however, a secret, which is as much a mystery to his wife as to his neighbors—viz, the source whence he derives his income. Making periodical visits to New York, he remains away but a short time and returns always with plenty of cash. The fact that he is known in that city by another name is first intimated to STELLA by MISS PRIM, an inquisitive old maid, and the certainty of its truth is subsequently confirmed by FRED TOWN, whose appearance on the scene evidently causes the husband great uneasiness. The wife being sent away, an interview between FRED and RALPH reveals the fact that the father of the latter has but just learned of his residence in Jersey and of the deception he is practising. A letter brought by FRED commands his instant return home; and, awed by the paternal summons, RALPH flies from Jersey, leaving a few hasty lines as explanation to his wife. MR. BILLY BUDDLES, who is spying in Eatentown for a certain purpose, obtains possession of the letter left by RALPH, and it is from his lips STELLA first hears of her husband's flight. The letter left for her reveals all his baseness, and informs her that their marriage was a mockery—that she is not his wife. In the moment of her grief FRED TOWN appears and offers her his friendship, and gives the real name of RALPH GORDON, as RALPH RANDALL, son of WALTER RANDALL of New York. The certainty of being utterly deceived, arouses all her strength, and accepting the proffered friendship of TOWN, resolves to make herself in the eyes of man what she is in the eyes of Heaven—RALPH RANDALL'S wife.

The second act takes place in the park of MR. RANDALL's residence on the Hudson. The curtain rises on an amusing collection of characters interrupted by the return of FRED TOWN from his sketching trip. MR. RANDALL being in quest of a housekeeper, FRED brings STELLA to fill that position, introducing her as Mrs. Lee. She is received by CORA ADAIR, a cold and haughty woman, with disdain. CORA, who is the protege of RANDALL, is designed by him as the future wife of his son. Securing the place, however, she again meets BUDDLES, who is RANDALL's man of business, but he is silent as to her identity, being under the influence FRED TOWN. MR. RANDALL informs CORA of his son's expected visit, and assures her that before his departure their engagement will be an established fact. During this time ELLA, RANDALL's daughter, who is engaged to FRED, becomes jealous of his apparent attentions to the new housekeeper, and thereby seriously endangers STELLA's position. The arrival of RALPH is followed by his proposal to CORA, which is overheard by STELLA and TOWN, closing the act with an effective tableau.

Act III. passes in the drawing room at MR. RANDALL's villa. MRS. MALVERNON, the aunt of FRED TOWN, calls on ELLA and CORA, bringing with her Miss PRIM, who is paying her a visit. STELLA suddenly enters in her character of housekeeper, meets Miss PRIM, and the surprise of that lady convinces CORA that there is a secret connected with STELLA's past life. Miss PRIM, yielding to STELLA's wishes, refuses to speak, and the visitors depart without CORA's curiosity being gratified. CORA has, however, seen enough to convict STELLA of deceit, and knowing of RALPH's residence in Jersey through the aid of BUDDLES, arrives at a shrewd guess of the truth. STELLA confesses to FRED TOWN the result of Miss PRIM's appearance, and it is agreed that STELLA must depart in order to avoid the dismissal which CORA will be certain to obtain from MR. RANDALL. At the moment she is preparing for her departure, she is suddenly brought face to face with her husband. An explanation takes place, and to his horror he discovers that the housekeeper he has heard of as Mrs. Lee is the woman he has so basely wronged. Carried away by her feelings, STELLA pleads with him to atone for his fault—she speaks of the old home and the old happiness, and with all a mother's love for her boy, begs of the man who should be her husband to give that boy a name. At first hesitating, he is upon the point of relenting, when CORA, who has overheard all, appears between them, giving to STELLA a letter from MR. RANDALL, dismissing her from the house. RALPH sinks back, and the curtain falls on a powerful and affecting tableau.

In the fourth and last act the scene remains the same as Act III. RALPH, having resolved to atone for his fault by marrying STELLA, confesses all to his sister, and bids her farewell. His father, in his blind desire to see his son the husband of CORA, the child of his old friend Adair, resolves never to forgive him, and, candidly informing RALPH of his intention to disinherit him, offers him two thousand dollars. This RALPH refuses to accept, and bids his father farewell. At this point, Mr. WIMBERLY, who has been the guest of RANDALL, endeavors to mitigate the anger of the stern old parent, and secures a meeting between him and STELLA. She tells him the story of her life—reveals the whole truth, and compels the old man to admit her entire innocence. While confessing that his son is bound in honor to make her his wife, he still refuses to see either of them again, and expresses his determination to divide his estate between his daughter, ELLA, and CORA, the child of his old friend Adair. STELLA, having obtained a full knowledge of CORA's past life through FRED TOWN's influence over BUDDLES, desires to be left alone with her, and the old man, being a listener at that interview, discovers to his profound dismay that he has been doubly deceived, and that the girl he has loved and sheltered as the daughter of his old friend Adair is but an impostor and a cheat. In the moment of his anguish at this revelation, his son and STELLA come to take their leave. The last remnants of his pride causes him a momentary struggle, but the feeling of the father rises to the surface, and all is forgiven. There are several other characters not material to the development of the plot, but being closely interwoven with its incidents, make an agreeable introduction.

www.ingramcontent.com/pod-product-compliance
Lightning Source LLC
Chambersburg PA
CBHW031243260626
47169CB00007B/2427